Song of the Cicada

Song of the Cicada

"Flushing Araby"

Ted Cleary

Silver Song Press

2023

Library of Congress Cataloging-in-Publication Data

Cleary, Ted, 1965—
      Song of the Cicada, "Flushing Araby"—1st Ed.
      p.   cm.

   ISBN 978-1-962895-00-2

        1. Ted Cleary—Fiction. 2. New York City—Social life and customs—20th century—Fiction. 3. James Joyce—Araby—Fiction. 3. United States Immigration —Fiction. 4. Flushing, Queens—Social life and customs—Fiction. 5. Adolescence—Fiction. 6. Infatuation—Fiction.

Published by Silver Song Press, USA
Cover design by: Mara Satori
Cover Image: *The Rauschenberg Test;* back cover: *7 Train Sunset*
Conceived in Queens; executed *sur le motif* and in the NYC subway
Designed in the USA; printed worldwide

Set in Garamond

TABLE OF CONTENTS

Song of the Cicada

"…and yet her name was like a summons to all my foolish blood."

JAMES JOYCE

1

The days when she did not come in were agony to him. Days, even weeks could go by without her coming in, but every day, every minute, he expected her to step in off the street and glide through the rows of fruit like a long-awaited ship appearing at harbor's mouth and then sailing to its berth between the piers. At quiet times, he would stand behind the register gazing out at the sidewalk, the sidewalk dancing with passing legs—only legs because the sun flaps were hung so low that he could see only thighs and calves and painted toes, like those of dancers behind a rising curtain.

At times Eugene felt such clairvoyant urgency, such bursting expectancy, that he was certain she would appear: he was sure she would appear as if summoned like a specter by some smoke-enwreathed oracle; she would step in out of the sun in her white shorts and tapered shirt, one arm hugging her violin case and the other reaching out to the waiting fruit. At other times, when his uncle relieved him at the register and Pasquale was on break, he would restock the display bins, rotating the older fruit to the top and laying a fresh layer on the bottom. At those times, when he could withdraw from customers and retreat behind the veil of his thoughts, he would gently place the fruit on the padded paper and wonder which one of these plums, which one of these nectarines, which rich velvety Georgia peach would she pick to make her own. He laid each blue plum down with the softest touch, as if lowering the fruit to her very lips as she lay in bed, as she lay on her side with one elbow bent, her hand supporting her head, and her face upturned to receive his offerings. He waited on her hour after hour, day after day, feeding her the sweetest, most succulent fruits as the sun beat down on the summer streets and the maraca hiss of a thousand cicadas rose and fell in the distant trees of Union Street. And when he bit into the plums themselves, the plums ripe with all the sweet savor of summer, the juice ran down his cheeks like tears.

2

The first time she had come in had been a fresh-scrubbed day in spring, a breezy day after rain, with a clear blue sky dotted with speeding clouds that plunged the street into shadow—and then light—as they sailed quickly overhead. The breeze occasionally lifted the hanging flaps on the awning, bathing the mounds of oranges, lemons, and limes in pure white sunlight, and splashing the ceiling with stained-glass ripples of red, yellow, and green. It was around three o'clock when she had come in, carrying a violin case; she paused before the fruit display to select a couple plums and a banana. As she leaned over the fruit, she tossed back her hair with an easy flick of the hand. Her face, untouched by either blemish or makeup, and framed by her long black hair, was as dazzling as a winter hill after a night's snow. He did not think that he had ever seen anyone so beautiful, and this even though every day there were streams of girls who came into his shop who made him feel awkward and breathless. But this girl with the violin, she was different. She was no bauble, no toy, no wide-eyed, blinking doll who chopped down the sidewalk with tiny, cute-girl steps—no, she was something real. She was as pure and beautiful as the bright April day that had brought her to him.

3

With a shock, he had recognized her that first day as Soo Yun Lee, Michael Lee's sister, the girl from the concert. She used to be called Grace some time ago but had gone by her Korean name since high school. She was now, he believed, a senior at Stuyvesant, almost ready to graduate. Her little brother Michael went to the local high school with Eugene but was only a freshman, so Eugene, a junior, didn't know him too well. The only reason why Eugene knew of Michael at all was that they were both in the Asian Club, although neither as very active members.

Eugene recognized Soo Yun from a concert he had gone to earlier in the year, in the winter, a performance at which his little sister's piano tutor had been playing as well. Soo Yun had sat in the first violinist's chair, her profile to the audience, her black dress cut away to expose her shoulders and arms, gold and warm in the light. All night he had stared at her, unable to unfix his gaze, helpless before her beauty. He was grateful that she was up on the spot-lit stage, right in front of him, where he could devour her image without apology or shame, without having to sneak sideways glances at her every few minutes—as he would have to have done had she been in the audience a few seats down from him.

As he watched her, he had the briefly troubling feeling that he had seen her before, he couldn't recall when—long ago, a raincoat, wet leaves—but before he could pursue the thought, the memory, the needling distraction, he

4

became wholly entranced by her playing—by the rhythmic grace of her bow arm, by the sweet sounds of her violin, by the honeyed song of her low notes and the whirlwind flourishes of her high notes that left him gasping. His response was immediate, direct—as natural and unthinking as a bird leaping into flight, a bud unfolding into flower, or a fist opening in sleep. At one point he had burst into applause of such passionate intensity, such frenzied clapping, that it was several seconds before he realized that the piece had not ended but had rather merely paused between movements.

There were a few titters and outright guffaws from the heads behind him, jerking Eugene back into the night— into his red cushioned seat, and itchy pants, and the gum on the back of the chair before him. He had sat the rest of the evening in a constrained and unhappy silence, feeling the flames in his cheeks and the mockery of a thousand eyes glancing off the back of his head.

4

After the concert, though, at home, away from the crowd, he was able to return to the contemplation of her image. As his mother served cake to his sister and grandmother around the tiny dining room table, he sat in his room at the edge of his bed, still wearing his dress shirt and jacket, reading and rereading the program, studying the name that delighted him there—the name of Soo Yun Lee. How pretty her name was, how elegant and melodic, like three bright notes on a piano: *Soo Yun Lee*. A much more musical name than the others in the program: Hazel Weintraub, Chandra Zuflack, Hubert Fish, Megan Mangan—their names so awkward and clashing, tangled and jangling like barbed wire nursery rhymes.

Soo Yun Lee, Soo Yun—yes, that's who she was, that's who—the rain, the girl in the car—the budding question from the concert answered in a burst: she was the girl he had glimpsed years ago after a party. He had been at a birthday party, a fifth grade one of all boys, some younger, a party where he hadn't known half the guests; it had been a steamy party—it was winter and rainy outside—and after the party—after the riotous hours of sugar and soda, after the sweaty grappling over violent video games—cars crashing and missiles exploding—he had been standing in the doorway, chilled, dizzy, feeling a little sick, waiting for his mother to come. He stepped aside to let others out, the night windy and black but red with taillights, and then Michael Lee had bounded by, laughing, in his bright yellow raincoat, and jumped into the back of a car. And as the back door stood open, Eugene saw, in the light of the cabin, a girl, a pretty girl, older than he was, her hair pulled back, but then falling down neatly over her shoulders. She was dressed formally, in a black velvet dress, as if for a recital, a concert, and she looked spent, even sad, and then the door closed, and the light went out, and he couldn't see her anymore.

He hadn't seen her again, not until the night of the concert five years later—nearly a third of his life—and in all that time, he had never really known anything about her, except that she was Michael Lee's sister, and that she was pretty, and that there was something about how she had looked that night—drained, gloomy—that matched his own sinking mood after the party, the abrupt crash after cake and hysteria, as he had waited in the jostling doorway with the rain blowing cold and tail lights flaring red on the street, waiting for his mother to come.

A night long ago, nearly forgotten. The memory had remained, undisturbed, buried, like a drowned face under water, never quite surfacing, but sometimes glimpsed when image and memory collided, such as at rainy bus stops in winter, bus stops loud with the hiss of tires passing on the wet street; at such times, the memory almost surfaced, but this night it had burst fully recovered onto his mind, a reel of lost film, everything recalled—the party, the wind, the clicking thud of the car door closing behind

Michael Lee—because this night he had seen her again, at the concert, he had seen her eyes sparkling with the passion of the music. And it was for her face, her face that had been printed three times in his mind—in the car, at the concert, among the summer fruits—that he waited for so expectantly each day at his uncle's store.

5

He thought of her so often and so intensely that he had burned out her image and was left with nothing but a washed-out ghost, a pale radiance, a mere suggestion of form amid foggy haze. Her features were lost to him: they had been bleached out like overexposed photographs, or like the sun-faded portraits of women in the shop windows of Flushing, their eyes and bangs and smiles mere hints of blue dissolving into warped placards of white. The more he strained to see her, the less he was able to; he was like someone peering across a darkened field to the edge of a nighttime wood: it was only by looking away from her that he was able to see her at all. It was when he was not thinking of her, when his mind had relaxed, that her image bubbled up unbidden: her face appeared with sudden clarity as she started from his sleep, as he picked through a box of apples, or reached for the soap in the shower.

And those few times that she did appear in the shop, appearing like a miracle out of the steely heat of the avenue, he gasped from the vivid presence of her, the freshness of her features, the perfection of her face and body; to see her again, she who had eluded him in his chases through his brambled dreams, was to revive his soul, to banish all his gloom and dread, like someone waking from a troubled sleep to see the morning sun shining through the trees.

6

Her image accompanied him even in places most hostile to romance. Wandering down Roosevelt Avenue on the long June afternoons, on breaks from the suffocating store, he would weave his way among the jostling crowds and see her face in the air before him as if from behind a veil of fine lace. Down the sidewalks he moved, sidewalks burning with midday glare, and yet he glided unruffled, a shadow across the sea. With her face before him, shining like a chalice, nothing bothered him, nothing disturbed him from his dream.

With perfect serenity, he sailed among and above the street life of Flushing: he sailed past the buses starting up with high-pitched whines, blowing their gusts of hot exhaust across his calves; he passed the sidewalk preachers proclaiming the good news of the Lord Jesus Christ through crackly megaphones; he passed the black men hawking watches two for twelve dollars at the bottom of Pigeon Alley. He lingered by the Peruvian street musicians playing their sweet airy tunes on pan pipes and guitar; he skirted the squatting Chinese ladies selling batteries, *bok choy,* and small green turtles swimming round and round their plastic bowls. He crossed in front of a homeless man slumped in the recessed window of a bank. He gave smooth and easy berth to the gently swinging feet of a man sitting on a wall, seemingly entranced and writing in a notebook, his heels bumping to some internal pulsing rhythm.

With the heat damp and close around his skin, he passed the pizzeria with its A/C grinding out even more heat onto the sidewalk, a heat dense with the smell of mozzarella and garlic; he stepped past the OTB parlor with its chain-smoking men in crooked glasses studying the racing forms and staring with brittle hope at the live feed from Belmont Racetrack; he glided around the small wide women hauling orange shopping bags and trailing two or three weeping and tottering children. He passed clusters of teenage Koreans in wide-legged pants and tank tops, their hair spiked and gelled, some with long blond bangs tossed back across the tops of their heads. They gathered outside the Gap, slouching and smoking, laughing or reaching for cellphones that chirped like merry crickets. Flipping open their phones, they answer: "What up, yo?"

He smiled on his walks now—he smiled because there had been times when he had bristled among the throngs of Main Street, times when he had felt hemmed in and harassed, harried by the noise and the fumes and the squealing of bus brakes; by the heat and glare off the cars jamming up the intersections; by the drivers pounding their horns as the lights turned from red to green and then back to red again, nothing moving, everything gridlocked, the pedestrians surging around the cars like the sea heaving and swirling around the humpbacked rocks of a strangled shoreline.

He scanned the faces of the crowds at the bus stops and saw written there the frustration and despair of lives sunk in annoyance and grief: agonizing jobs, bullying bosses, kids gone wild and wrong; shiftless husbands, leaking toilets, and a nameless ache in the bottom of the soul. The crowds slumped on street corners, weary and waiting for the light to change, so ground down by the noise and grind of their daily lives, by the daily round of jobs and trains and swollen feet, by the crowding noise of TV, talk shows, and inane deejay chatter that they could no longer hear— if they had ever heard it at all—the deep hidden heartbeat of the world. Dulled and deafened by the frazzling din, they had lost all compass of their spiritual cores; they had become sealed off from their cool caves of meditative calm, those places in the heart where rest and relief were possible—where, in Eugene, the image of Soo Yun burned like a votive candle.

7

I t was at about this time that the posters for Queens Day began to appear on lampposts and bus stop shelters—blue and orange posters promising two days and nights of music and dancing, food stands and flea markets—the annual festival held down in Flushing Meadows Park, in the shadow of the giant globe left over from the 1964 World's Fair.

He'd been there a couple summers ago, before he'd gone to work in his uncle's store, and the one thing he recalled—besides his aimless, penniless wandering among the smoky barbecue stands and gift stalls—was that he wanted to return some day with a girl. Girls were everywhere at Queens Day. He had brushed by hundreds, thousands, as he had woven his way among the crowd—girls with hoop earrings, dark lipstick, and chests that shook when they laughed. White shorts, brown legs, little plump strips of belly between shorts and shirts. The girls were walking with their arms around their boyfriends—guys with gold chains, ratty mustaches and belts studded with beepers and cell phones; they wore their hats backwards and their shorts halfway off their butts.

Among the smoky stalls, girls and guys surged and eddied, pausing for shish kebab, or to shoot a row of grinning clowns' mouths full of water. Girls wiped zeppole cream from their mouths or bit into hotdogs, leaning forward to keep the mustard from dripping onto their clothes. Thousands of couples walked around the big central field, hand-in-hand, laughing, joking, and kissing.

The festival seemed the perfect place to go with a girl—the perfect place to go with Soo Yun—a place for them to get lost in the crowd, away from the searching eyes of mother and father, family and friends, a pair of minnows aswim in the warm green anonymous. Perhaps he could shoot three basketballs in a row, sink them all, and win a prize—a blue bear, a pillow heart, or anything else she wanted—something that she could take home and keep in her room. He could walk around with her, her hand in his—his hand a little damp—and then on the far side of the park he could maybe kiss her under the trees.

He carefully removed one of the posters from a bus stop and taped it to the back of the cash register, where the customers, and she, could see it.

8

Eugene's Uncle Jeong, for whom he had been working the last two years, summers and weekends, gave the impression of a soldier who had survived a terrible war and was therefore beyond worrying about petty things. Not that he radiated happiness, either. He just took a stoic middle course, steering among the joys and misfortunes of life like an old sailor navigating among reefs and rocks, shallows and sharks, unmoved by any of them. He permitted himself a few moments of levity around Christmas and the New Year, when, snug among the family, he sat at the smoky *kalbi* table, one bony knee across the other, and tipped back shots of *soju* until a grin spread across his face.

He ran a good shop, clean and efficient, keeping a close eye on Pasquale and the other help, but also treating them well, and fairly, so that they returned year after year. Although he didn't say much—he said very little, practically no more than was necessary to run the business—there were times when Eugene saw in him a kind of silent wisdom, the kind that a man gains when he has grown beyond the need to fill up the world with his noise.

There were times, especially in the late afternoon, when the six o'clock rush had died down, and the sun was sinking down behind the stadium, that Uncle Jeong came out from behind the register to stand downwind from his peaches and smoke a cigarette. With his shoulders slightly hunched and his eyes squinting against the curls of smoke, he regarded the ebbing tides of people as they trudged home to dinner, their clothes wrinkled, their hair limp, and their faces drained of whatever freshness they had shown in the morning. Eugene sometimes joined him to look at the crowds queuing up for buses at the close of the day.

"Life is work, sacrifice," his uncle had once remarked, flicking away his cigarette. "Once you realize, you'll be free."

Eugene might have considered his uncle a much wiser man—even a sage—had he not married a glittering bird-like woman who was still trying, at her advancing age, to cling to the sparkle of her youth by getting her hair and nails done every week, buying bright, tight clothes, and gossiping with her friends twice a month over coffee and tiny desserts at bakeries when she could have entertained for free in the fully remodeled kitchen she rarely seemed to use. She had sold her own nail salon several years before because the chemicals had given her headaches and she had not really worked since. She worked an occasional afternoon behind the register at the store, where she made no effort to hide her impatience and continually called out to Eugene for the prices of everything.

One time, a few years ago, she had gotten five out of six Lotto numbers and had won over ten thousand dollars, which she had immediately spent on an expensive Japanese karaoke machine and a huge crystal chandelier— a full five feet across—that hung menacingly over her dining room table like a gigantic growth of stalactites.

His aunt and uncle had no children of their own, so that is why Eugene worked at his uncle's store, getting paid a little less than minimum wage—but he was paid half in cash, so it wasn't bad, and he liked his uncle, so he didn't complain. It could have been worse, like some of his friends, who worked for family and weren't paid at all—at least not with money—but rather with dinners or gift certificates or "free" clothes from the store (the price tags still on them so they could do the math)—a currency of some value, perhaps, but try taking a girl to the movies, or a coffee shop, and paying with a gift certificate from a

Korean restaurant, or with a pair of black sweatpants—try doing that, and see how far that gets you.

9

I n his room, with the door closed and the fan thrumming, Eugene sat staring at the following listing in the phone directory for the Asian Club:

Michael Lee 718 493 6929

Michael Lee: Soo Yun's brother. The yellow rain jacket from years ago. As Eugene stared at the number, he was awed by the knowledge that if he were to call those seven digits, he would be able to speak to her. He would be able to hear her voice on the other end of the line. But naturally, he had no legitimate reason to call her—or her brother for that matter—so all he could do was sit and stare at those numbers until he saw her name just beyond Michael's, a ghostly *Soo Yun* blinking on and off through Michael's name like a neon shop sign flashing, alternately, in blue and gold: Bar, *Sushi*, Bar, *Sushi*. Michael, *Soo Yun*, Michael, *Soo Yun*.

He saw her phone number pulsing behind his eyelids when he went to bed at night, and he often murmured the number to himself like a quiet prayer: 493 6929, 493 6929. The number became enshrined in his mind and he couldn't pass by a phone booth without thinking of her. The phone in his own home was torture to him because there was only one and it was mounted on the wall outside the kitchen, where any conversation could be plainly heard by anyone—except, perhaps, by his half-deaf grandmother who sat inches from the blaring television, leaning forward, a teacup chattering nervously on the saucer balanced in her lap.

No, any call to Soo Yun would have to be made from an outside line, preferably from someplace shielded from street noise, behind glass and out of the rain. On his late afternoon walks around Flushing, he kept his eyes open for likely phones and had staked out several promising places, among them the lobby of the bank, a Chinese restaurant, and the Koryodang Bakery.

10

Often at night, to get out of his close, crowded house, Eugene went walking. It was the only way for him to be alone with his thoughts. Even if he were to shut himself into his room and wedge a towel into the crack under the door, he would never get any peace. The door and walls were so flimsy and thin—composed of molecules so far apart that they seemed to challenge the very notion of solidity—that they could do very little to muffle the television or the shrill random complaints of his mother. Nor was the bathroom any refuge—no quiet shrine of chrome and white tiles—it too had a cheap door with a rattling, broken lock, and someone always knocking—usually his grandmother. Because of her nearly endless cups of tea (twenty-two in one day, his sister had once counted)—and because her bladder was tiny and weak—she was almost always in the bathroom, on the way to the bathroom, or just shuffling back from the bathroom.

To withdraw to his room and blast music through headphones—the usual retreat of the young—was no help either: flat on his back, sweaty, with the damp and sticky headphones clamped tightly to his ears—this was no rest, no asylum. He was pinned by pounding drums and screeching guitars, by the strident shrieks of singers whose problems weren't his own: their problems, not his, spat out in coarse and unwieldy rhymes. Some of the lyrics came close to expressing something—half a refrain or a turn of phrase—but no sooner was something being said— something with a glimmer of meaning, a breath of truth— than the mood was instantly broken by a sudden time change or a pointless rant about something else. Eugene hungered for a deeper music, something that would more fully address his longing and sadness, but he hadn't found it yet, and until that day—and to hasten that day—he would have to spin his own music, to become the master of his own song, and to do that, he took to the streets, a dragon uncocooned, and walked, and walked, and walked.

By walking out alone, he could be with her. He could conjure up, from the very rhythm of his walking, a life with her, which he could then savor and observe, suspended and swinging before him like a lighted paper lantern. Images, bright, silent—shifting brilliancies—visions of calling her, kissing her, strands of hair damp on her temple, their immediate unspoken union; and then, a few years later, after college, their wedding: a sunny green garden of top-heavy peonies (their unopened buds like globes for wandering ants); cousins and uncles with green Fuji cameras, and in the blurred slanted photos (even the ones half-browned by handbag straps), her face, beautiful, and his, bright with happy confusion.

Like a guitar player finding a groove, strumming some chords until the shape of a song emerged, or like a potter at his wheel, pedaling, pressing, spinning the clay, shaping it, squeezing it, whirling it round into the waist of a woman, so did Eugene conjure up, from his spring-driven heart, a love and a life with Soo Yun.

"When you go at night, where you go?" his mother would ask.

"Nowhere," he said, "just walking."

"What you mean, just walking?"

He shrugged. "Just that," he said. "Just walking."

"You mean you don't meet with somebody, friends?"

"No, just me."

"You mean you just walking? No *PC Bang?* No billiard? No karaoke?"

"No, just walking."

At first, Eugene's walks worried his mother: where she came from, people didn't "just walk"—not at night at least—they walked because they had to. When she was a child in Korea, in her village in the mountains, she had to walk two miles to school—the hill path was too rocky for bicycles. She carried, in her shoulder bag, her books, her lunch—*kimchi* and rice—and, in the winter, wood or coal for the big iron stove in the schoolroom. This walking to just walk—in this country, at night, New York, who knows what could happen: gangs and kidnappings and crazy people—strange white men, unshaven, serial killers with vans.

When he would return, often hours later, after midnight, or even at one or two, she would be "just up," watching TV with worried eyes, or sponging down the kitchen counter; either that, or she would suddenly coming out of her room in her night dress to use the bathroom, intercepting Eugene on his way to his bedroom, studying him closely, even sniffing him, as she did to bottles milk to check if they had gone bad. But Eugene had nothing to hide: no bloodshot eyes, no cigarette smell, not even the bright minty mask of chewing gum. No sweet and strange smell of marijuana, that pointy leafed weed she had seen on magazine covers warning of the dangers to America's youth, yet another night-beast to destroy the futures of her children—sex and alcohol and guns and school shootings; maybe she should have just stayed in Korea, where things were harder, yes, but simpler: just crashing economies, corrupt politicians, and the lingering threat from the North.

She examined him, and sniffed him, and questioned him, but as he never came home smelling of anything, nor bumping unsteadily through the door, nor hunched in the back of a police car—and as he didn't cause any trouble or miss any work—she got used to his night time walking, the same way she got used to the pains in her fingers and ankles, or to anything else she couldn't do much about, finally accepting it as one of the eccentricities of her adolescent son. He was that age after all.

On his walks, Eugene zigzagged north and east out of Flushing to Bayside and Bay Terrace, sticking to the residential streets and staying off the hot and noisy main drags—Northern, Francis Lewis, Bell Boulevard—the big avenues with their raucous clots of teenagers leaning up against cars—low-slung sports cars with booming amplifiers and bright violet neon around their license plates.

He preferred the quiet back streets of houses and trees, and walked down the center of these streets, between the lines of the sleeping cars, and the rhythm of his thoughts would fall into line with the rhythm of his walking. He strode down the center of these streets, their moist and leafy darkness punctuated by intervals of light: the orange light of humming streetlamps, in whose brightness wheeled a flittering cosmos of flying insects: little gnats like dust, and flies, and great shaggy moths wings fluttering and thumping against the light. Some of the flies—whizzing miniatures—made quick, tight revolutions of the lamp, and then, after their brief, bright orbits, shot back into the gloom beneath the trees, their sudden illuminations like the brief lives of souls between their two eternities.

As he walked from lamp to lamp down the streets, his shadow lengthened, and then faded, as the light behind him failed; and then, when he came upon the next lamp, his shadow was suddenly born anew—squat-shouldered, vigorous, with bold black lines—but then that too would lengthen, with every step, into a fantastic long-legged taper of gray, a carnival creature; it would lose its shape amidst the motley of leaf shadow, but then, just when it would seem to have lost itself completely, to have dissolved forever, his shadow would spring back to life again—bold, black, a resolute silhouette, striding with squat and muscular purpose north and east.

His goal was the water; instinctively it was always the water. The rhythm of the walk has its own fluidity, its own momentum, and when the body stops, the mind still needs a rhythm to hook onto, to propel it, to support it—like a soloist, the rest of the band having dropped out, playing a cadenza over the silent beat in the break; it is the implicit rhythm that keeps things going. So at walk's end, when he had his feet over the rail and his face to the warm steady breeze off the water, Eugene's mind rolled on, buoyant, bobbing, supported by the roll of the bay in the dark oily water.

At the end of his walk, northeast in Bay Terrace, he climbed the footbridge over the Cross Island Parkway, its six lanes loud with traffic and spinning rubber, and entered the narrow strip of park by the waterside. Early in the night, the bike path was busy with skaters and joggers, teenagers on bikes. Heavy women walked by with big tee shirts and spandex shorts, their chins held high, gripping CD players like discuses in their swinging hands.

He left the bike path and walked far out on the banging planks of Bayside Marina, past the clubhouse and glowing soda machines, past the solitary fishermen leaning with their elbows on the rail, their stringy hair straggling from their baseball caps; he walked out past all the rods slanted out over the water, through the gauntlet of fish guts and filament line, broken bobbers and rusted lures; he stepped around buckets of bloody water, some swishing and flailing with fishtails, the evening's catch. He walked out to the very end of the pier, to the last rail whitened by seagull guano, and sat down with his feet off the side and looked out over the bay.

He gazed out over the water, over the shifting darkness streaked with lights, at the red and green beacons of the piers and the boats out on the bay. The hulls of the boats were as ghosts on the water, rising and falling in the gentle swells, and on the heaviest of summer nights, when the air and water were at a dead calm, the boats were as pale and still as tombstones. But when the wind picked up, ruffling the black, the colored streaks squiggled across the water like luminous snakes, or neon flagellates swimming eastward in a warm and fertile darkness. He looked across the bay to Douglaston, to its dark and broad mass spotted with lights, its hundred houses shining through the trees. He tried to guess in which house she lived—that one there, with the golden windows on the water, or perhaps that other one poking through the trees, there was really no way to tell. But eventually his eyes would choose a house, and he would stare at it across the water, and sometimes when he stared, the bobbing of the boats and the swell of the water made it seem as if what was bobbing was the land, and not the bay—and he would see the hill rising like an ocean liner, all its lights ablaze.

He fixed on a house, that one there would do, and wondered what she was doing inside, what she was doing—yes, she was in her living room, alone, listening to music, one leg slung over the arm of a cushioned chair, her screened windows opened to the night and to the breathless puffs of wind coming across the water, and she had her head back and eyes closed, listening to piano music. In her hand was a tall glass of ice water, beaded with condensation—some of the beads had even collected and run down the side like streaks of rain on a car window—and the glass was wet and cool against her thigh, against the bare skin of her leg. As the music played, she slowly rolled the bottom rim against the skin of her inner thigh, rolling and unrolling the coolness, and when she raised the glass to her lips, the crystal tinkled with ice cubes.

Her house was quiet, except for the music, and the whispered lapping of tiny waves on the pebbled shore. The music was a nocturne, an adagio piece for violin and piano, pedaled and full of resonant open voicings, and at an especially slow and spacious part, she turned the music louder, so the wires and the wood, the coiled strings of the concert grand, filled the whole house with their resonance and overtones; she turned it even louder and closed her eyes and smiled, and his eyes dwelled on her eyes, and her hair, and on the curve of her cheekbone as it swept down to her lips; the piano wove chords, an undulating web of sound, and then a violin entered, embroidering a line of luminous gold; it smoothly soared and dipped, stitching her name to the dark skin of his heart.

As the music played on, the texture of his dream, his gaze left her face and eyes; it left her eyes and lips and swept down her neck and across her breasts; it glided over her shoulders and then out along the bare skin of her arm to sweep up to her hand, her hand with its palm upturned like a lily; her fingers played in the air, it played the strings

27

of a violin whose honeyed song drew his heart to hers, which called to him from across the buoys and black waves of bay.

11

One Friday afternoon, while delivering two bags of groceries to an apartment on Union Street, he saw her through the smoked windows of the Koryodang Café. He stopped short in front of the hairdresser's, the two plastic bags of melons, peaches, onions, and greens wobbling and bumping against his leg, his gaze fixed at an oblique angle across the sidewalk to the corner table of the café, where she sat, hand on chin, gazing dreamily out the window.

She appeared more serene than the other women waiting in the window, women sitting with their handbags in their laps, checking their watches, glancing every few minutes towards the big parking lot, within whose congested, gridlocked expanse glittered a thousand windshields, each burning with a fiery white spot, each brilliant point like a welder's torch in the hot summer sun. He dared not speculate whether she was waiting for a girlfriend or a boyfriend; the dreamy look on her face made him uneasy.

He had stopped in front of a beauty shop that had a mirrored pillar; it greatly pained him to see his soiled jeans, skinny chest, and unruly, humidity-crazed hair. His sneakers were collapsing, broken by so much standing, walking, and humping packages through the streets of Queens. It was not for a body like his that Soo Yun was sitting in that café dreaming. He might have stood there longer, scowling at himself with disgust and loathing, digging at himself like someone picking at a scab, scratching deeper for blood, were it not for his sudden noticing that the hairdressers inside the shop were giggling at him and covering their mouths with their hands.

He turned away abruptly, the day suddenly noisier and hotter. He stepped off the sidewalk and out between the strangled, honking cars, cutting across Union Street before even reaching the corner, not wanting to pass in front of the café for fear of being seen by her in his dirty shopboy clothes. Or, even worse, to be *not* seen by her, to be seen right through like the smoggy air, even as he passed before her very eyes. As he reached the other sidewalk and caught his reflection anew in the staggered windows of a streetside lobby, seeing his image ripple large and small against the uneven face of the building, he knew that he was so plain, so unworthy of even the briefest lingering glance, that he would never even brush up against her consciousness; his was just one of those thousands of sidewalk faces that she passed every day without noticing.

12

A few days later, after a long day of work, with his weekly pay and all his other savings in his pocket, he walked down Roosevelt Avenue to a clothing store with towering photos of moody, tousled-haired models pouting in the windows. After some hesitation on the sidewalk, some crossing back and forth in front of the door, he committed himself to going in.

Inside, he was given a discreet but thorough once-over by a thin black security guard who then, perhaps judging Eugene not to be a shoplifting threat, nodded slightly and returned his gaze to the sidewalk outside. Farther into the store, in the air-conditioned inner sanctum, neat stacks of tee shirts awaited him, along with stacks of jeans and khakis—tan, olive, and blue. Overhead, small, tilted speakers pulsed out a tinny, machine-driven dance beat: *dum tikka dum tikka dum tikka dum.*

Insensibly, not knowing what he was looking for, Eugene wandered among the displays while long mirrors gave him back his grimy and diffident reflection. He shied away from the colorful fabrics, overwhelmed by all the choices, wishing he had an older sister or brother who could just take charge of him and say, with total authority, *Look, Eugene, this is what you need to be cool.*

No point in thinking about that, however—he had no brothers and his sister was only twelve—so after wiping his hands, he tentatively touched the material of some of the pants.

"Can I help you?"

To Eugene's left, a salesgirl with golden nose stud was straightening up some shirts. "You looking for something?" she asked.

"Me?" said Eugene. "No, just looking." Then quickly, he added, touching the pants in front of him: "How much are these?"

"Those?" said the girl. "Says right there, $39.99."

Eugene nodded thoughtfully, as if judging that a fair price—the price that was printed plainly on the red and white placard—and stroked the fabric again between thumb and forefinger.

The girl finished with the shirts and came closer. "You getting them for your girl or something?"

Eugene stared at her.

"I don't understand," said Eugene. "My girl?"

"Because," said the girl, smiling slightly, and dropping her voice into a whisper, "thems is girls' pants."

Eugene felt himself blush, which didn't help him at all, because he immediately blushed even more. He felt stricken, with red and singing ears. Mercifully, though, the girl did not laugh, but merely smiled, and beckoned to him with a kindly finger.

"Come with me," she said. "I'll hook you up. I know just what you need."

After about forty minutes of numbly acquiescing to the girl's suggestions; smiling uneasily at her compliments ("You looking sharp now, honey. *Superfine*."); and trying on endless shirts and baggy pants—pants so baggy his legs were lost in them—he left the store with a bulging bag of clothes, feeling dizzy and relieved, hardly remembering what he had bought. He had spent nearly everything he had saved since May. It was closing time, and on Eugene's way out, the thin security guard nodded once more—the terse, inexpressive nod of all doormen—and locked the door behind Eugene, the key chain clacking sharply against the glass.

"Now just you get a haircut," the girl had said, "And *all* the girls be after you."

13

T wo nights later, after he had gotten a haircut, a spiky doo that flared above his head like a gelled mace, a weapon of war, he called her. He really did. The feeling had been building all afternoon, a feeling like the deep charge of an approaching storm, like a rising tide, the feeling that this would be a significant day. His smart new clothes also seemed to call for action. He phoned her at exactly nine o'clock, when he got out of work. It seemed like the perfect time to call because dinner was sure to be over and no one was likely to have gone to bed yet ("Who is that, calling at eleven? I'm up at six."). Also, if she were watching TV, there would be nothing on yet. It would still be commercials. He had planned it perfectly.

He called from inside the Koryodang bakery, in the vestibule, a good place to call because it was screened from the noise of the street and from all the busy chatter and cup clinking inside.

A simple pretext for calling had occurred to him the night before: he would simply call pretending to want the number of another kid in the Asian club, Nathan Lee, whose name was printed right below Michael's on the list. It was perfect, innocent, admirable, all under the guise of school spirit. The way he planned it, he could perhaps call a few more times and then, after becoming friends with the brother, he could engage Soo Yun in conversation and pretty soon maybe he could arrange to meet her right here at the Koryodang bakery, where he had seen her a week or so before gazing out the window. That was her table over there.

Her table was empty at the moment, and as he regarded it, spacing out—the moment lengthening and the dial tone droning in his ear—he peopled it with two images: first, hers—dreamy, elbows on the table—and then his: attendant, charming, regaling her with tales of Pasquale and Uncle Jeong, grandly buying her a fruit tart or a second cup of cappuccino, if that is what she wanted.

As he watched the spectral conversation shimmer beyond the smoky glass, he experienced a dizzying doubleness—and then tripleness—of vision: atop his imagined self, assured and debonair, he suddenly saw his actual reflection: lizard crested and mesmerized, mouth half open in reverie. And then, atop these two, flashed the image of his former unkempt bag-toting self, his outgrown skin, his chitinous shell, bewildered in the hairdresser's window just days before.

If you would like to make a call, please hang up and dial again. If you need help, hang up and--

He dropped his quarter in the slot, punched in the seven numbers, and focused his entire attention on the earpiece. His heart bumped around his chest like a bowl in a box.

She answered on the first ring.

"Hello?"

It was she. Soo Yun. It was *Soo Yun herself.*

He was staggered. He had not expected this. He had been prepared for three or four rings and then, at most, a conversation with the brother. But not *this,* not a one-ring pickup and then *she herself.*

"Hello?" she said again, into the silence, one *hello* away from the querulous tone of one who is beginning to think she might be dealing with a crank.

He jumped in before it was too late: "Oh, hi," he said. "Is Michael Lee there?"

"Who should I say is calling, please?"

Her voice was beautiful, polite. He loved the way it sounded in his ear. It was soft and classy, smooth, the lining of a cello case. He could barely comprehend that it was she who was on the other end of the line, holding a receiver to her ear, the same way that he was standing in this elated café, holding a receiver to *his* ear, talking to *her.* It was a beautiful thing.

"Hello?" she said again. "Are you there?"

"I'm here," he said, like a simpleton.

35

"I'm sorry," she said. "But who should I say is calling?"

"Oh," he said. "A friend of his from school."

He could hear her sigh but she, perhaps realizing that it wasn't worth the effort to coax anything more detailed out of him, put down the phone and walked off to get her brother. He pressed the phone tightly to his ear. He could hear her slippers sliding briskly across a polished wood floor, become muted by a deep piled rug, and then pick up their sliding on the other side. The room was huge, palatial, and she was wearing a white terrycloth robe. She arrived at the bottom of the stairs, placed one hand on the banister, and called up to her brother.

"Michael. Mi-chael!"

A muffled reply came down the stairs.

"Phone call!" she said.

A door opened upstairs, and music spilled out.

"Who is it?"

"I don't know."

"*Who?*"

"I don't know," she said, irritably. "He didn't say. Just pick up."

By this time, Eugene knew he had made a terrible mistake. This call was no good. He had sounded like a moron and now he was just bothering everybody. Then, in a terrible flash, he suddenly realized that it was idiotic to be calling to ask for Nathan Lee's number because it was on the *very same sheet of paper* from which he had gotten Michael's number—printed right below it, in fact—so if he had Michael's number, he should have had Nathan's, too.

He slapped the receiver down before he caused himself any more embarrassment. The phone shot a bolt and gobbled his quarter. He pushed through the door and hurried head down through all the smartly-dressed people waiting outside, everyone dressed in black, checking cell phone messages or shaking their watches free from their jacket sleeves to verify the time. He disappeared into the crowd, his white jeans obliterated by sharp brushstrokes of black.

14

Near the end of July there was a thunderstorm every afternoon at about five o'clock. Every day the steam built up over the course of the morning, mounting steadily with the heat, following the sun as it climbed like a blinding heat gauge into the hard silver of the sky. By noon the day was unbearable, hot and damp as a dog's breath, and the heat from the streets slapped him in the face as he rounded the corners of sun-hammered avenues. In the haze-blunted light, the trees cast no shadows, and the leaves hung limply like the heads of mourners awaiting the passing of a hearse. The shrill tidal swells of cicadas rose and fell in the endless afternoons.

And then, every day, after the sticky morning and stifling afternoon, after the sun had pounded the streets into a tarry soup, the steam gathered into thunderclouds, each one black and green like an ugly bruise; a little before five, when the humidity had reached its fullest heated bloom, Eugene would step down off the pallets behind the counter, and stand at the mouth of the shop, just in under the awning, waiting for the storm to break.

He heard, in the moist and breathless dark, the cry of a bird from a few streets over; then came the sharp smell of radiators, the smell of rain-fried sidewalks carried on the wind. Next came a few large, scattered drops, spattering fat and dark like drops of oil, disks of paint, and then, with a great whoosh, like a door opening into a wild afternoon, the wind gusted in from the west, whipping up dust and scraps of trash, and rippling the kite tails of all the grand opening pennants and streamers on the avenue.

Then the first lightning crack: the shatter of a tree splitting from crown to root. The darkness split in its rippling glare, its veins hot and white, a tree root cast in streams of silver magma.

On the street, people ran for cover, newspapers over their heads, or clutching umbrellas that flapped like shattered crows; they ran into the shelter of stores and then turned to watch the storm. Eugene made way for the people ducking into his shop, raindrops streaking and dotting their clothes, and nodded at them with the sudden intimacy of those sharing a spectacular sight.

Girls jumped in, drenched, excited, their tee shirts dripping, the skin of their shoulders showing wet and fresh through the fabric. In twos and threes, they hugged each other as the thunder crashed all around them.

Eugene stood just in from the fluttering and dripping awning, waiting for her to come in, willing her to run in and take shelter in his arms. He waited, barely breathing, his arms almost trembling, waiting for her to duck in with her rain-soaked blouse and violin case, waiting for her to run into his arms. He was sure that was all it would take. He was sure that once she was in his arms, once she was snug up against his chest, her hair black and wet like strings of beads—once she was there, she would turn her face up to his and he would kiss her. He would not hesitate. He would just kiss her. To wait even a second would be to lose her forever.

So day after day when the rains came, he stood at the shop front, waiting, and day after day she did not come in.

He stood with half-closed eyes, trying to summon her from the street, like a sculptor seeking to release a woman from a dream of stone.

At the end of ten days, the weather broke and the storms stopped. She had not come in even once.

15

On one of those days, in the hours before the rain, Eugene had been cleaning up the fruit displays, ripping out the stained and squashed layers of tissue paper and cardboard. The old packing was stained and dimpled from the bottoms of peaches and plums, and little squibs of juice had dried in gradations from their outer fringes to the inner, looking like mountains on a topographical map. He replaced all the box liners, swept off the tabletops, and then—with a quiet diligence that drew a thoughtful glance from his uncle—dragged out the tables (groaning, wobbly) and swept up in the dark places behind them, places where the broom seldom reached.

After sweeping up some dust, a hollow cicada shell, and the dried silky strands from ears of corn, Eugene spotted, in a crack between the floor and wall, in some unexplained crevice, a green and white shoot emerging into the light. He was about to stab at it with the bristles, to scrape it out, when he checked himself and laid down the broom. He knelt down and leaned forward to better see. The shoot was from a potato that had fallen down behind the display stands, fallen down into the dust and dark among the crisscrossing legs; it had sprouted, out of its wrinkled hide, pink and white shoots, one long and the others small, and was bending them up out of the crack. The shoots, like bumpy and knuckled fingers, were pink and white with a little green at the tips, where they had caught a little light through the weave of the burlap and the gaps between the planks.

The potato had been in the hole for weeks, for months, long enough to have been eaten by mice, by insects, or simply to have dried up and rotted, but instead of shriveling away and dying, it had grown shoots and roots, white threadlike hairs that searched out dust from potatoes and onions, carrots, and the dried shucks of corn. With its rough skin and pink-white arms, it looked like something primal, ancient: a sea creature, a spiny coral, a fantastic barnacled crab.

He marveled at this strange thing, this simple tuber, that from its hole had twisted and squeezed itself towards the light, towards life. It seemed wrong, unnatural, after such an effort, to just tear it up and dump it in the trash, so he eased it from the crack, and later, on his way home from work—after glancing around to make sure no one was looking—he planted it in an untrampled spot on the verge of a small park.

16

A few days later, taking care not to dirty his new white pants, Eugene was in the stockroom with Pasquale, restacking sacks of potatoes. He was swinging a bag when he saw—snapping into focus through the drinks cooler—Soo Yun, with a tennis racquet under her arm, choosing among the bunches of seedless red grapes.

Pasquale turned to look. "*Ah*," he said, "*su novia. La Bonita.*" He articulated the three syllables of *bo-ni-ta* with particular clarity and emphasis. He winked and took the sack from Eugene. "I finish, no worry."

Eugene quickly wiped off his hands and swung open the door to the shop; he recalled stepping out on stage in a fifth-grade play. He eyed her helplessly as she leaned over the fruit, one leg extended behind her for balance. He stepped up behind the counter, told his uncle he would relieve him for a few minutes, and took up his spot behind the register. He shot himself a quick look in the mirror mounted behind the headache and heartburn remedies, and Soo Yun laughed.

"You really want to get that?" she asked.

He jerked around, a rush of blush to his cheeks. Another voice—bright, male—jumped in.

"Sure," said the voice. "She'll love it. You know how little kids are, they love sweets."

To Eugene's right, by the candy rack, stood a Korean in a golf shirt and white shorts, holding up a big swirly lollipop almost the size of his tennis racquet. His voice was bright and cheery as sunny California.

"This," he beamed, "is probably the finest lollipop I have ever seen."

Soo Yun smiled.

"Well," she said. "It *is* her birthday."

Eugene turned away, unable to look at her. His ears had begun to shut down and he felt himself shrinking into a coiled ball in the back of his brain, a fetal tuck in the whorl of his soul. Out among the fruit, Soo Yun and the boyfriend chatted on with their sunny banter, their words like tennis balls batted lightly across the courts of a country club, a private demesne where everyone wears white, and then retires to the cool green lounge for crystal drinks and slices of lime.

He wasn't hearing them, though: their voices had become indistinct behind the muffling traffic and car horns. He felt weak, faint, as he used to when he was hungry and tired and about to pass out at church as a child; the world receded into a pinpoint tunnel of gauzy seashell noise, and it was only by steadying himself on the counter that he was able to remain standing at all. He kept his eyes averted as he rang up her things and placed them in a bag. And she, judging from her upturned palm, the way she chatted over her shoulder as she waited for the change, was not looking at him either.

After Soo Yun and her boyfriend had left, Eugene returned to the stockroom, his head down and eyes extinguished, and Pasquale, straightening up from his labor, turned to him with a joke on his lips. But seeing Eugene's face, he gave him a sympathetic nod and got out of his way.

17

That night, with the fan blowing hot air over him and rippling the hair of his arms, Eugene lay awake, revisiting the painful afternoon in his mind. He did so despairingly, helplessly, compulsively playing it over and over, just sharpening the hurt and humiliation, just etching it more deeply into the mind. The sweet elegance of Soo Yun at the grapes, the helpless lift of his heart, the fatuous laugh of the boyfriend. Eugene bristled at the boyfriend's cavalier entry into the store—his braying banality, his toothy cheer— a tourist bursting into a cathedral upsetting the prayerful quiet.

Eugene's mind whirled with dreams of murder. He had a sudden vivid fantasy of seizing the boyfriend's tennis racquet and beating him with it, beating him with it until his head split open like a watermelon—until his head split open and spattered the whole store—ceiling, floors and walls—with pink wet flesh.

The next day after work, his mind still churning with vengeance, Eugene walked north on Main Street and stomped upstairs to a *PC Bang* where, in a shadowy room pulsating with house music, a crowd of teenagers was intently playing war games on computers. Battles burst across the screens and headphones crackled with machine gun fire. Hunched in black cushioned chairs, the players aimed and swiveled their animated gun barrels, fingers clacking away.

Eugene logged on, selected the map of a stone desert fort with serrated mountains all around, and, in a mood for mayhem, entered a game as a terrorist. He threw himself into the fight boldly, almost recklessly: no body armor, no hacks, no tiptoeing around, no cowardly camping out behind the big green boxes. No, he went right to it. He rushed down halls and through half-opened doors into the open, leaping side to side, hopping over walls, and shooting up everything with his nasty weaponry. He slaughtered the enemy with precise and explosive violence: he grenaded them backwards over the parapets, chopped them up with the machine gun, and whacked them cleanly with the sniper rifle, its crosshairs zeroing in for a headshot every time.

Eugene was deadly, unbeatable. After a few hours, with some kids swiveling to look at his screen ("Mad skills, yo."), he had racked up 131 kills and had been killed only twice, and then only by some worm of a camper who had staked out a spot behind a green box in an out of the way tunnel. The coward had hidden in the shadows all game, listening for gunfire and running feet, and then shot Eugene when he ran past the box, bomb in hand. The same camper spoiled the next couple games until Eugene made an example out of him by sniffing him out and cutting his head off with a Bowie knife.

Eugene did this in game after game, giddy, entranced, slicing the head off in a geyser of blood; and the fifth time around, when the head had rolled to a stop face up on the flagstones, Eugene saw with a shock—and then base elation—that the head belonged to Soo Yun's boyfriend, the sunny Californian with the perfect teeth. His grin, bloodied and broken, was no longer so dazzling. Flies soon found the head, nimble greenbottle flies. They tiptoed to the wounds and dipped their forefeet into the blood, washing their hands like emerald priests.

Eugene hunted him down in game after game, and Eugene killed him in creative and various ways: with the machine gun, the knife, headshots with the Glock. Even with the bomb itself, jamming it under his chin. It got so bad that California shrieked at the very sight of Eugene, dropping his gun and running off with his hands fluttering over his head like some comic book sissy in a tizzy. Scampering off in his tennis whites screaming for his mother. Coolly, after letting him run, Eugene steadied his aim and dropped him from one hundred yards.

This orgy of blood, however, this frenzy of killing, gave Eugene little satisfaction. He had gone to the *PC Bang* craving the fever and purgation of violence, but the more he murdered the boyfriend, the more he shot him, the more he sliced him open from navel to chinbone, the sicker he felt. Finally, after several hours, after the day had long since gone, Eugene stepped out into the street, drained, ten dollars poorer, no happier than he had been when he had gone in.

18

A s he walked home, in the darkness streaked with taillights, Eugene felt the same sad and sinking emptiness he had felt two winters ago when he had cut school to avoid exams. He had gone as far as a subway ride would take him: all the way down to the southern tip of Manhattan, to the end of the 1 train, and then had spent a long and aimless day on the Staten Island ferry, grinding back and forth across the wintry New York Bay, its dark waters brightening in patches of silver as the sun shone down from between gaps in the clouds.

He had thought the day would bring him freedom, out on the expansive Bay, under the arm of the Statue of Liberty, but it had left him feeling empty, as empty as the grand and abandoned midday ferry, its three humming decks painted teal and turquoise—teal on bottom, turquoise on top—a color scheme that guiltily reminded him of the hallways of his school. The great wooden benches were set out crosswise like church pews, warm wood against the cool blue-green, and on the benches slumbered men in big woolen hats, sleeping with their arms folded and the *New York Post* slipping off their knees; homeless men picked through the garbage bins and jangled up and down the stairs with plastic bags filled with cans; and down on the lower deck, the vibrating bathroom smelled of bleach and urine and its three toilet stalls were shorn of doors.

He had stood hunched by himself on the rear deck, hands jammed in his pockets and his eyes watering from the wind. Seagulls hung in the breeze behind the boat, hoping for scraps of hot dogs or potato chips, carried across the bay in the tumultuous, swirling after draft of the ferry.

Now, a couple years later, he thought it strange that he could remember that day on the bay with such vividness, such clarity, when so much time had passed and he hadn't thought much about it. But it was as if his gloom had opened a portal in his bottommost mind, a trap door with a view down into a vortex, a vortex in which spun, and sank, and buoyed up again, his private, totemic images of sadness.

19

He came home the next afternoon to find his little sister crying at the piano. She was alone in the house. It was a Wednesday, and their grandmother would be at the community center with her friends. His sister appeared not to have heard him come in and was seated with her head down, hands in her lap, whimpering to herself. Her small shoulders shook beneath her thin white shirt.

He halted for a moment on the living room floor, not knowing what to do, whether to leave her alone, for fear of embarrassing her, or to try to comfort her, which he had little practice in doing. He had always thought of gloom as his own private domain. This was something new. As he looked at her, his little sister, he realized with a flush of shame that he did not know her at all. She had always been the model daughter: respectful, quiet, straight A's since kindergarten; she sang at the church, danced ballet, and practiced her piano for an hour a day without being told. All her life, she had been perfect, proper, almost unnaturally so—as opaque as the fine china his mother kept behind glass in the dining room cabinet.

She had grown from an infant to a little girl to a perfect glasslike lady all in a couple years when he wasn't looking. But now she was twelve years old and crying, sitting alone at the piano in an empty house. Finally, after suppressing the impulse to retreat to his room, he coughed lightly into his hand to announce himself. When she started, he walked up behind her, and after a moment's hesitation, laid a gentle hand on her shoulder. She looked up, and then turned away, her lower eyelids rimmed with tears. He sat down next to her.

"What's the matter?" he asked.

She shook her head. "Nothing."

"What do you mean, nothing?"

"I don't know."

"But you must know. People don't just cry for no reason."

She shrugged.

They fell silent, and in the silence, one punctuated only by her sniffing, he looked at her hands in her lap and at the eighty-eight piano keys laid out before him in half steps and whole steps, black and white, so orderly and arranged. Major and minor chords were articulated like geometry, and in the tiny cracks of the black keys, the brown of the wood showed through. Some of the keys in the tenor clef had been worn down by use.

He opened his mouth a few times to say something but no words came out. A tear rolled down her face and splashed onto a piano key. He sat looking at it, at the tear drop, at its black splash of wet on one of the small keys. The only other sound other than his sister's sniffing was the air conditioner droning in the other room.

A few minutes passed and he still said nothing. He started a few sentences in his mind, a few words of solace, but he abandoned them all because they sounded false and lame. In the end, he said nothing.

When her crying died down and her breathing was no longer catching itself in short jerky gasps, he stood up and laid his hand one more time on her shoulder. She was no longer shaking.

"You all right now?" he asked.

She nodded and gave him a tiny smile. When he was back in his room, standing quietly, the door still open, she stretched out her fingers and began to play.

20

A few nights later, after watching a long movie on video, one of his sister's favorite's—and for which Eugene would have to confess a secret liking—he dreamed of Soo Yun. He dreamed he was in a crowd at harbor side, seeing off passengers on a towering ship. It was a long time ago, and the men wore hats and women wore dresses that they had to catch up at the sides when going up stairs. She was among those climbing up the gangplank; she wore a white dress and a pink ribbon in her hair.

The crowd was waving handkerchiefs and calling up to the rail with cupped hands, but the great horn of the four-funneled ship blared and drowned out all other sounds in the harbor basin. The deep organ blast echoed across the water and up against the warehouses, the shipping offices, and the houses on the hill. All other sounds ceased to exist: the rattle of trams near the quay; the shouts of shop boys and the cries of fishwives; the hammer and clink of machine shops; even the piercing shriek of the train whistle in the wharf. All were dwarfed by the great bellow of the ship as it prepared to heave off to sea.

He thought he saw her at the ship's rail, leaning over and looking down, biting her lip, searching among the faces in the crowd for his. He tried to wave but his arms were pinned tightly by the crowd; he was pressed in by men in wool coats, smelling of dampness and beer. Flecks of tobacco blew into his eyes his ribs were too crushed to breathe.

Finally, he got enough air into his lungs to cry out her name, but his voice was lost amid the other voices, and then they were all drowned out by the sailors' shouts and the portside whistles and a final blast of the ship's horn as it was towed out to deeper waters. The ship, its four black funnels soaring, was towed by a pair of tugs, each churning a frothy wake as they labored under the colossal weight of their tow. In a few minutes, the ship had been swung around and was pointed to the gap in the harbor's mouth.

One final sounding of the horn and the ship was under way, trailing gulls in the air behind it. As the crowd began to scatter, making its way to the trams and pubs, he was able to reach the harbor's edge. He rested his ribs against the rail and gazed westward for a long time, watching the ship shrink into a speck beneath a ragged plume of smoke.

21

Finally the day came when she returned to the store. It was about two o'clock, the sunlight was blinding outside, and she was standing at the register in white shorts and sunglasses, shaking some change out of her purse.

Eugene rang up each of the fruits—a nectarine, a plum, and a peach—and sneaked glances at her as he punched the numbers in on the scale. Though only a few feet from her, he despaired at the gulf between them: the gulf between his desire and her untouchability. She could have no idea of the hours and days and nights he had thought of her, of the millions of billions of neural flickerings that had shivered through his brain, generating her image endlessly, like lightning quickening in the heart of a cloud. She could not know that in front of him—at all times, sleeping or waking—was the image of her, hovering and ghostly like a hologram.

"That's $1.79," he said.

"Okay," she said, and poked among her change. She smiled and extended her hand.

"I hope you don't mind all these coins."

"Not at all," he said. "We can use them."

He reached for a small bag. *Keep the banter going. Small talk. Ask her a question.*

"You're Michael Lee's sister, right?"

She looked up in surprise. "Yes," she said, "I am." Her tone was as much questioning as answering. She seemed to be seeing him for the first time.

"I go to school with him," Eugene explained.

"Oh," she said.

"Good guy," Eugene added.

"He can be," she said. "Sometimes." And then she smiled, nearly paralyzing him with its kindness.

He could barely open his hand to pick up the fruit. He had a clear memory of himself as a boy, about age five, on ice skates in the park. He had fallen on his stomach, his breath knocked out, and he had, for several seconds, been staring at the ice, unable to breathe, unable to cry.

"So," he said, struggling off the ice. "So how did that birthday party go?"

She looked at him, not understanding.

"Birthday party?" she said. "What birthday party?"

55

"I don't know whose, really," he said, a little flustered. "Some little girl's, I think. You were in here the other day with your—I think, boyfriend, or some guy—buying a big lollipop—"

She brightened. "Oh, I remember now. The lollipop. That was for our little cousin." And then, as if to clarify, she added: "That was my cousin, not my boyfriend."

The words had left her mouth but were not immediately comprehensible to Eugene. They were like words floating to him from another language: *Her cousin, not her boyfriend.* Then, as he began to register their meaning, to understand, he stared at her like an OTB stooper staring at a winning triple exacta. His heart expanded so forcefully that it almost blotted him out. An immediate surge of spirits— her cousin, not a boyfriend! Relief, contrition, hope: a turmoil of emotions, jumbled recollections: his painful bed, bloody video massacres, aching ships. No time to dwell, though—he had to ask her. Ask her!

Trying to keep his head from exploding, he leaned over and tapped the Queens Day poster. He spoke carefully. "Hey, Soo Yun," he said. "Are you going to Queens Day?"

"Queens Day again?" She peered at the poster. "When is it?"

"August 11th and 12th," said Eugene, placing his hands on the counter to keep them from trembling. "It's coming up."

"August 11th and 12th," she said, thinking, touching her sunglasses to her bottom lip. "August 11th and 12th."

As he watched her, his eyes pulsing almost painfully, Eugene rehearsed his next line, one he had polished in countless reveries, perfected over countless miles of midnight pavement.

"If you'd like to go," he'd say, "I'd be honored to take you."

Then he would smile, suavely, but humorously, as if he knew that Queens Day was a very modest date—the nightclubs of the city would come later, when he was more established, when he had a driver's license and credit cards—but for now the Queens Day festival would be a good place to start—a walk in the park, some easy laughter, maybe a kiss. A start at least. Then she would smile, and he would smile; and then she would lower her eyes shyly, and that would be the beginning of the rest of his life.

That was how he had dreamed it, how it was supposed to happen.

Finally she spoke. "Oh, I'm going to miss it: I'm going to be in Korea. I'm leaving in a couple days."

Eugene said nothing for several seconds. And then Princeton, the fall. That was it. The speck and the rail and the seagulls.

But you can think about that later.

"Oh," he said finally, lamely. "Korea." The word was like a slab of stone across his heart.

"Yes," she said. "With my church. Also to visit my aunts." She scooped up her little bag. "Thanks," she said, and started for the door.

He called after her.

"Oh, Soo Yun," he said.

She turned around. He tapped the poster again and smiled weakly.

"I'll get you something from the fair."

He couldn't be sure that she had heard him because she only smiled in a confused way and raised her paper bag as if in the way of a salute.

"Bye bye, now," she said, and left.

22

The days between her leaving and Queens Day were interminable and dull—hot and gray, and unbroken by any relief or rain. He walked to work among buildings that cast no shadow in either the morning or afternoon. The trees along the streets hung their heads like mourners awaiting a lumbering hearse, a hearse heaped high with wreaths and flowers, flowers wilting in the noonday heat. In the slow times between customers, he would stare at the calendar, with its maddening empty squares of white—the prison cells of his days, a dry honeycomb, his queenless hive. He attended to customers with a sleepy lethargy, barely looking up at anyone, or at the bags that he absently packed. Even the door, the usual portal of his soul, held no hope for him because he knew she would not be walking in.

At night, in his room, he held a globe in his hands, tracing his finger west to east from America to Korea: he traced it across the merry patchwork of the American states—the quilt of pink, yellow, and green—from New York to California. He then traced his finger up and over the broad blue expanse of the northern Pacific, arcing it under the curve of the Aleutians and the Siberian islets, and then swept of south over Hokkaido, Honshu, Shikoku, and the Sea of Japan to the mountainous peninsula of Korea, within whose ragged borders were contained the entire focus of his soul.

As he gazed at the bold black bullseye of the capital city, he imagined her down among the many millions, among the noise and smog of August, amid the cars and motor scooters and tottering old people with short legs and facemasks tied across their mouths as though they were bewildered old surgeons who had wandered from their hospitals into a different century.

Soo Yun was down there, with her camera and handbag, crossing plazas with aunts and uncles, posing for photos before temples and grand monuments from the last war, photos that would end up in albums filled with other identical photos: rows of miscellaneous relatives, shrunken to near invisibility, lined up before statues, monuments, or famous vistas, either backlit into silhouettes or squinting blindly into the glare. He saw her smiling politely and bowing to relatives. Great aunts and uncles leaning forward to hear that this was Soo Yun Lee, the daughter of Chung Lee and Ji Won Im, who was, of course, the daughter of Yoo Ri, the aged woman's sister. *Yeh yeh.* The pretty young American who would be going to Princeton University in the fall—*Ivy League.*

He closed his eyes and leaned back in his chair, permitting himself the fantasy of flying into Seoul with a suitcase, khakis, and sunglasses, and then bumping into Soo Yun quite by accident at Changdeokgung Palace, in the cobbled plaza before the two-tiered main gate. She would pause, shocked, and then she would laugh and smile, her face brilliant with recognition. He would say that he had come for her and she would throw her arms around him and they would slip away from the aunts and uncles and spend the afternoon with each other, alone, in the secret gardens beyond the lotus pond, on their backs beneath the trees of the park, their fingers intertwined, nuzzling and talking. They would have so much to talk about because they had never really spoken before.

One night his mother intruded into his room in the middle of one of his reveries, and when she asked him— her eyes narrowed with shrewd suspicion—what it was that he was doing with that globe every night, he looked up and coolly told her that he was memorizing all the countries and capitals of the world for the Global Regents, and while one of her eyebrows remained aloft in a skeptical arch, his answer seemed to satisfy her and she withdrew.

After the door had clicked shut, he resumed his contemplation of the small Korean peninsula, his eyes half-closed and a smile on his face, knowing that somewhere down there she moved and laughed and stretched and slept.

23

T wo days before Queens Day, after the excruciating slowness of the preceding days, Uncle Jeong surprised Eugene with the apologetic yet terse request that he work until 10 pm on Saturday night and most of the day Sunday. His wife had just reminded him that they had two weddings to go to—the daughter of his wife's cousin on Saturday, and the son of a close friend on Sunday.

His uncle must have sensed his resentment, his sudden spike of anger.

"You tell me, I know," he said. He frowned and looked out on the sidewalk. "I'm sorry. I try to get back early on Sunday."

When Saturday finally arrived, he worked glumly, looking out from under the awning at the thousands of legs scissoring by on the blazing sidewalk, envying their freedom, their musical clicking of clogs as the girls walking on their way to meet friends, some arm in arm, their long strands of bleached hair gelled and hanging down on front of their eyes like characters out of Japanese animation.

Sunday was spent the same way, but with less torture, some hope, because at least he would be getting out early, by six at the latest, which would give him a good three or four hours to make a few loops of the whole place and hunt down something special for Soo Yun. Most of the good things would have probably sold out by then, but six o'clock was better than nothing at all.

He spent the day in his white pants and shirt (with the collar turned up), and with the gel melting from his hair and oozing down slowly over his forehead. Several times throughout the afternoon, he reached into the napkin case, folded a couple into a wad and carefully wiped them across his brow, mopping off a dirty line of sweat and grime.

At five-thirty he began to tidy his hair in the tiny gap of mirror visible between the mouthwash and tampons, and looked expectantly between the shop front and the clock. By six-thirty, Uncle Jeong had still not shown, and by seven—even in the briefest gaps between customers— Eugene was striding impatiently out past the orange bin to search up and down the block. The sun was slanting low, sinking behind the church, and was shooting its rays, golden and oblique, along the northwestern faces of shops on the avenue. He peered at all the faces coming into view, searching for his uncle's head bobbing towards him in the crowd.

Eight o'clock, then nine.

At exactly 9:16 by the big bank clock, a car pulled up at the curb. The back door opened and a man's dress shoe and ankle touched down upon the ground. A little more conversation and laughter. After a merry round of parting *anyunghi kesehyos,* Uncle Jeong emerged and entered the shop. His face was red and his leg brushed up against the orange display, knocking one to the floor, where it then rolled with a slow wobble out the door. Eugene could interpret these signs. He was too angry to greet him.

Behind the counter, Uncle Jeong slowly took off his jacket and carefully arranged it on a hanger. He brushed some dust off the collar and sleeves with the backs of his fingers.

"Sorry for late," said the Uncle. "We are delayed at party."

Eugene slowly exhaled his anger out his nose.

"Can I go now, Uncle?"

Uncle Jeong raised his eyebrows in surprise, two red circles on his cheeks.

"You want to go now? Festival still open?"

"For another half an hour."

Uncle Jeong blinked, then shrugged.

"Okay," he said. "You work all day. You want to go, you go."

Eugene looked at the cash register.

"If it is no problem," he said. "Can I get paid for yesterday and today? I want to buy something at the festival."

Uncle Jeong frowned as he thought, his eyes a little glassy. He pursed his lips as if to whistle, and then looked at Eugene.

"Yesterday and today?" he said. "Yes, okay."

He opened the register and pulled out a bunch of twenty-dollar bills. He peeled off three and laid them down on the green cigarette mat. Then he laid a fourth on top.

"Tip," said the uncle. "I have party. Now you have party."

24

H e ran toward the 7 train, leaving Uncle Jeong and Pasquale behind him. He dodged down the sidewalk, trying to worm into his jacket as he ran, but one of the sleeves was twisted and he couldn't get his hand in. To hell with it: too hot anyway. He rolled it into a ball, tucked it under his arm, and dodged in and out of the sidewalk crowd like a football player sprinting downfield. Customers stepping out of Uncle King's restaurant stopped short and stared after him, too surprised to even shout. A quick glance at the digital clock over the bank read 9:33. He was absurdly late. The escalator was broken on Roosevelt Avenue, so he bounded down the grooved and littered steps two at a time, leaping over scraps of newspaper and assorted trash—McDonald's bags, OTB tickets, coffee cups—all the way down the seventy steps to the cavernous, white-tiled underground station. He slid his Metrocard through the chrome turnstile and saw the dull, blood-colored train waiting on the center track. He raced around a column and hopped on, tucking himself in like someone expecting the train doors to shut abruptly behind him.

He need not have rushed. He still had to wait another ten minutes, his blood pounding in his head, for the train to shudder awake, for the conductor to test the crackly PA—*testing one two testing*—and for the cars to lurch out of Main Street towards Shea Stadium. In the time he waited, he strode angrily through the cars, even permitting himself a bad boy swagger, yanking open the doors with a violent rattle as he made his way to the front of the train. At the front, pressing his forehead up against the glass, Eugene stared out the scratched window at the tracks crisscrossing before merging into the one local track stretching westward to Manhattan.

He was thinking that he would have been better off to have run west down Roosevelt Avenue, down over the bridge spanning the highway and the poisoned waters of Flushing Creek; down past all the junkyards and auto wrecks, the piles of hubcaps stacked a mile high; past all the windowless warehouses and assorted rubbish of Queens; he'd have been able to run the whole mile and a half faster than it was taking this train to get started.

It was 9:52 when the train finally reached Shea. As it rushed into the station, Eugene's eyes jerked and glided over the crowd waiting to get on—a crowd happily exhausted, laughing, bobbing with big stuffed bears, balloons; women's wrists glowed with bracelets of neon green.

Eugene was the only person to get off.

The park was emptying out and the last few streams of stragglers were lazing towards the exit: couples arm in arm, the woman's head resting on the guy's shoulder, a pleased smile on her face. From far off in the park, beyond the trees and green, the jingly chimes of the Mister Softee truck reached his ears, its *pop goes the weasel* melody warped and distorted by the distance.

He jogged on into the park, crunching on plastic cups, following the curving paths towards the globe and rockets. A pack of teenagers was bopping up the hill, baggy pants and stockings on their heads, all walking in the same rolling strut, *like they was bad, real bad.* As Eugene was passing them, one of them burst towards him, flicking his fingers like flashbulbs right in Eugene's face, yelling, "Boo!"

Eugene jerked away from him and ran on, the mocking hoots and slapping high-fives receding behind him. One of them yelled "Yo! Yo!" and took a few slapping steps in pursuit but then gave up, laughing.

A little farther on, he passed through a wrought iron gate, on whose spikes had been impaled, in all positions, a menagerie of carnival prizes: clowns, stuffed animals, and splay-legged dolls. On a large corner spike, next to a kebab of impaled oranges, sagged a unicorn with pink ribbons in its mane.

By the time he got into the heart of the park, where the vendors and trucks had ringed the vast open middle, a few cop cars were slowly circling the perimeter, droning over their loudspeakers for everyone to keep moving towards the exits and that the park was now closed. Garbage was everywhere: papers, bottles, bags, streamers, raffles, burst balloons, and cheap toys already broken and discarded. A girl was crying under a tree. At the big bandstand in the middle of the park, workers were dismantling the spotlights and scaffolding, and as Eugene looked on, the flags and tarpaulins came tumbling down. At stage front, another team of men loaded speaker cabinets onto a truck.

A police car approached Eugene, cruising slowly, the driver's elbow jutting out the window.

"Park's closed, guy," said the cop.

"I know, I'm leaving," said Eugene, and hurried on.

25

Over to Eugene's right, rap music blared at him through distorted speakers. A stand appeared to still be open, though empty. Radiating outwards from its roof were several streamers hung with pennants emblazoned with the call numbers of an FM radio station. There was some laughter behind the shack and a woman came bouncing in, looking behind her. She was dark-skinned with bleached blond hair and a leopard skin top. A grinning guy in a tank top and razor thin sideburns reached in and tried to pinch her spandex, but she slapped away his hand with a laugh.

"Not with you, never. Go find a hand to play with." Then she saw Eugene approaching and waved him off. "Sorry, yo, we closed."

26

T *he park is now closed. All persons must proceed to the*
nearest exit.

He hurried around the perimeter of the park, ignoring the cops, not holding out much hope for finding anything good. Nearly all the stalls had been completely dismantled and were rattling by him inside large, rented trucks, the trucks stuttering and whining as their drivers struggled to find the next gear. Eugene walked down a slight decline, passing an old man coming up the hill pushing a hot dog wagon, its small wheels rumbling on the concrete. He was a tiny man, pushing the cart with his back bent and his arms straight out, a figure from ancient mythology.

Eugene stopped and surveyed the whole park, shielding his eyes from the lamplights. Resentment boiled up in him like black water. There was nothing to buy. Nothing. He had come to a fair that had hosted a quarter million people but had showed up too late to buy anything.

But then, before his rage could rise too much to choke him, before he could tilt his head back to scream, he spotted, under the widespread arms of an elm tree, an Indian family loading wares into the back of an old 1970s station wagon. He could hear the dull thunking of jugs and the tinny clatter of bronze platters. As he approached, he saw through its windows the lips of vases and the handles of tall, long-necked jugs. Even though the car was in shadow, Eugene could see that the wares were elegant: antiqued bronze and tin, intricate ornamentation, delicately painted pottery.

The father of the family, his face dark and gleaming above his pale blue shirt, struggled to the car with a heavy box. He plunked it down on the tailgate, where a thin brown arm reached out and slid it farther into the car. The man raised his arms in a half-shrug and wiped each of his cheeks against his sleeves. He had big sweat stains under his arms.

"So hot!" he said. "As bad as India."

He ran his fingers outward along his eyebrows and shook off the sweat.

"Almost," he added, correcting himself. "There is nothing as bad as India."

He waved vaguely at the wares inside the car. "You like to buy something?"

"Maybe," said Eugene, peering in the window.

"You will have to look fast," said the man. "The police."

"I know."

"Look, look, around the back here. I have good things. Made by masters in Rajasthan."

He wiped his face again and beckoned to Eugene. "What are you looking for? What do you want? See these vases here, you like this vase? Or these elephants? Feel the weight of them. Mahogany, pure mahogany. And the carvings, look: that is quality."

As Eugene examined an elephant, the man pulled out another box.

"I have swords, too. You are looking for swords?"

"No swords," said Eugene.

"No swords? No elephants? You are hard to please, no?"

On the far side of the park, the lights started to shut off, plunging large pockets of grass and trees into gloom. The cop on the PA droned on in dull, plodding tones.

The park is now closed. All persons must exit immediately.

"You will have to hurry," said the man.

"All right," said Eugene. "How much are those? Those vases, jugs, whatever they are?" He pointed to a box of nicely made urns, slender, with large whorl-shaped handles sweeping out from the bottoms like ears. They were gold, red and black, lacquered, with floral designs, but also illustrated with pictures of elephants, tigers, and figures in turbans.

"Those are thirty-five dollars each."

Eugene kept his money in his pocket. "I think I'll pass."

"You don't like? Why not? Who is this for? Your mother? Your girlfriend?"

Eugene hesitated, and the man laughed. "Ah, your girlfriend, right? Right? How did I know? Ah, look, you're smiling. You're smiling. I'm in this business a long time, and I was in other business before this, a special business, a …well, a business. So I know love when I see it. Love, this is a beautiful thing. A very beautiful thing. And I have something for you, perfect for you—Arjun! Give me that box there!"

The man slid the box out onto the tailgate and, with his hand on the box top, paused like a magician about to unveil a miraculous sight.

"But first," he said, leaning towards Eugene, "you must tell me something." His voice had dropped: he had something very important to say.

Eugene waited. Yes?

"You must tell me," said the man, scrutinizing Eugene— "You must tell me whether this girl, this woman—" Here he shook his head, as if at the inadequacy of his language. "What I mean is—" and here he paused again to search for the right words "—do you love her—and please forgive me if I can say this no better—do you love her with all your body and all your soul?"

Eugene looked sharply at the man, looking for a trace of mockery, but didn't find any.

"I am completely serious," said the man, drawing himself back, stung. He frowned at Eugene, disappointed. "I see. You think I am some carnival salesman with honey talk, saying anything to sell you something. To cheat you. But that is not it."

He sighed, like someone always misunderstood, and looked out over the darkening park.

"In this life," he said, but Eugene cut him off.

"Sir," said Eugene, "I didn't mean—"

The man waved him off, but kindly, as if he understood that people like Eugene couldn't help themselves— couldn't help their blundering, their rudeness.

"Listen," said the man, and placed a finger to his lips. "Sometimes it is good to just listen." He looked away for a moment, intently studying the gloom. Eugene looked too, and for a few moments, they were both staring across the field at the distant circling police car. With his fingers, the man drummed on the roof of the car, making a sound like running horses. When he spoke again, he seemed to be speaking to himself more than to Eugene.

"It seems I am cursed to do this forever," he said. "But I cannot refuse. I cannot refuse because it is the nature of the art."

He turned back around and carefully studied Eugene. "Tell me this," he said, and then spoke quietly, seeming to find a deeper rhythm. "Do you love her," he said, "so deeply that you wake up in the night weeping and saying her name?"

The intense earnestness of the man's eyes prevented any suspicion of insincerity. Eugene said nothing, holding the man's gaze. When the man spoke, his voice was low, assured, comforting. He was like a good doctor, a priest. He seemed to suggest, to recognize, that although the festival was over, and the lights were going out, and the cops were hurrying them to leave—he seemed to be saying that Eugene's needs were more important to him, were worth the risk of any summons. He asked something else, his voice still quiet:

"Tell me," he said, "do you love her so much that the touch of her skin against your skin is like the shiver of wind in mountain cedars?"

In the pause, Eugene nodded.

"Do you love her so much that in your dreams the rivers of your blood mingle with hers and the two run as one to the sea?"

The man's voice was starting to become more impassioned.

"Yes," said Eugene.

"Do you love—"

There was some giggling inside the car.

"Hey!" the man shouted, pounding on the roof. "*Chup!* Shut up in there!"

His passion had flared into anger. He glared at Eugene like a mad prophet.

"Do you love her?" he demanded.

Eugene couldn't talk.

"Do you love her, I said! Not as a boy loves, *but as a man?*"

"Yes," said Eugene helplessly. "I do. I do love her."

"As a man?"

"Yes, as a man."

"A man!" he yelled.

"Yes, a man."

"OK, then, OK," said the man, relenting, finally satisfied. He closed his eyes and breathed deeply several times before opening them again. "Then this is for you," he said quietly. "This is for you and your lady."

He began to lift up the lid.

"And there is no need to look at anything else."

When the man opened the box and lifted out the vase from its nest of tissue papers, Eugene knew, even in that poor light, that there could never have been a more beautiful thing made by the hand of man.

It was a large jug with a deep rounded bottom and a strong middle shaft that widened toward the top. There were two sinuous handles on the sides that arched and then curved back towards the base. The vase had the same rich colors of the other vases: red, black and gold, but also had various inlays and dancing figures that he couldn't quite make out.

He imagined giving it to her, giving it to her in some place of candlelight and roses. Her face would brighten, as if splashed by sunlight—at first with surprise, and then with gratitude, and then her suddenly kindled love—as if the fire he had been trying to ignite in her heart had finally caught, bursting up from its damp, smoky heap like a genie from its fabulous bottle.

"How much," said Eugene. "How much is it?"

The man sucked a long draught of wind through his nose. He took his time in answering. "This," he said, "is a very special piece. Very special. There can be no bargaining on this piece."

Eugene waited, looking at the sweat accumulate on the man's upper lip and roll into his mouth.

"There can be no bargaining," the man repeated.

"I know," said Eugene. "I understand."

"I sincerely hope you do, said the man. "It is—has to be, no exception—one hundred and twenty dollars."

Immediately: Fear. The aching speck, gone, the ferry.

"But I only have eighty," said Eugene.

"I am sorry," said the man, "but it must be so. It is one-twenty. There can be no exception." He shook his head sadly and began to place the vase back into the box.

"No one understands," he said. "This is made by Rajasthani masters, great artists who spend their lives—"

More lights shut off around the park.

"—first in apprenticeship and then in caves up in the mountains—"

He delicately arranged the tissue papers like frills around the neck of the vase.

"—Many go blind from the intricacy of the work, just a few inches is—"

Eugene thrust his hand deep into his pocket and pulled out his damp and crumpled twenty-dollar bills. He held them out in sincere supplication. The words spilled out of him.

"Look, please, sir. I have only eighty dollars. Eighty. I work in my uncle's store and get four dollars an hour. There is this girl who comes in the store, her."

The man slowly shook his head. "I am sorry," he said. "Please understand. I have bills to pay, rent, children—"

Eugene's words gushed on, spurting.

"She comes in, she comes in, and I don't know what to—what am I supposed to do? She's older than me and in the fall she's going, she's going to college—"

The man raised his hands in an attitude of surrender, still shaking his head. He closed his eyes, too, as if it were too painful for him to listen to such a story.

"Since the beginning of the world—" he said, sadly.

Eugene dug into his other pocket. He held out a subway fare card as if it were inscribed with holy verse.

"Look, please, sir, I have a Metrocard," he said. "I'm not going to lie to you, it has only $8.50 on it, but that's almost ninety dollars all together. Please, sir, *please*."

Eugene's squeezed-out vowel hung in the air for a few seconds and then the man relented, lowering his hands from the surrender position.

"All right," he said gently. "You win. I give it to you. Give me the money and the Metrocard."

He took the money, and the card, and shook his head bemusedly as he straightened out the bills. He seemed to smile at his own foolishness.

"Of course, I have no head for business," he said. "Do you know why I have no head for business?"

Eugene shook his head, no.

"Because I cannot keep these things back. I give them away, these artworks." He put the money in his pocket.

"But I can't hold back such art from someone in love. That would be wicked. Sinful. It would be against the spirit of the artworks, of life itself. Such things should be given freely."

Reverently, he lifted the box and handed it to Eugene. "Treat this," he said, "as you would your woman."

Eugene took the box into his arms, carefully—more carefully than he had ever taken anything into his arms— as if Soo Yun herself had fallen out of the sky and into his embrace.

"Thank you," said Eugene, "thank you so much." And then, all around the park, the last of the humming lights snapped out to black.

27

Eugene had no money or train fare so he had to walk home. He didn't mind. He felt so giddy he could have run home laughing. But he couldn't do that. He was on Roosevelt Avenue in a sketchy neighborhood, a gloomy stretch of bus garages, train trestles, and auto graveyards, and he would have to stay wary-eyed until he made it back to the bright gas station lights of College Point Boulevard. He didn't want to get jumped and have his treasure stolen—not now, not when his quest was almost at an end.

Roosevelt Avenue was deserted except for the occasional car that banged across the broad metal plates thrown over the pitted roadway. Alone on the sidewalk, Eugene started across the long iron bridge that spanned the dark and stinking waters of Flushing Creek, its surface wiggling with reflected streaks of light and broken by half-sunk pylons and shopping carts. When he was halfway across the bridge, a train lumbered overhead, heading to Main Street, swaying and screeching on the rails and sending down a shower of blue sparks. In the tricky spasms of light, in the flickering blue fireworks, hooded muggers appeared and disappeared in the huddled shadows of girders, slipping away into puddles of urine and pigeon feathers. Eugene shivered but sped on, his scalp stiffening, looking back every minute or so.

When he started up the grade to College Point Avenue, towards its traffic lights and towering gas station signs, he began to relax, to breathe more easily, and deeper. The end of the tunnel, almost there now. With his every step, the vase bumped lightly inside the box, clunking gently with a cozy murmur.

28

With a surge of confidence, he emerged from the long grade of the bridge into the light of College Point Boulevard, into the noise and traffic. Once on the other side, in the brilliant—even blinding—glare of the Mobil station, he felt the urge to look at his purchase again, to admire it, and to confirm that he had done the right thing in buying it.

He stepped over to the base of the giant sign and, after cautiously brushing off the dirt and tiny pebbles, sat down on the concrete pedestal. He laid the box on the ground between his feet, pinched up his pants to relax the cloth, and carefully removed the lid. He then reached down into the box and lifted out the vase with the tenderness of a new father lifting an infant from its cradle.

Once again, he was dazzled by the design and colors, which now, unfortunately, in the stark gas station light, seemed perhaps a little busy, a little garish—but perhaps it was just the overhead light: too harsh, too white. What did the Mobil people, after all, know about how to light the work of the Rajasthani masters? The masterworks of artists who spent their lives in caves, going blind from the intricacy of—

My God, no. There's just no way.

The vase slipped into the box, falling, cracking dully like an ostrich egg. He stared disbelievingly down between his feet, as if through a portal to the underworld.

He stared for at least a minute, during which the traffic light, with deliberate humming clicks, changed from red to green and back to red again. He then ventured his hands into the box and lifted out the vase again. There was a thin but noticeable crack extending from the base right up to the pouting lip, where it had knocked out a chip of finish. But that is not what concerned him.

What he couldn't believe were the pictures—the pictures are what he couldn't believe. *Nearly every square inch of the surface was devoted to pictures of people fucking.* There was no gentle way to say it—that's what they were doing: plain and simple fucking. Or, actually—to be more accurate—very contorted and inventive fucking. In the rounded portrait areas, what in the poor light of the park he had mistaken for people dancing were actually men and women in all kinds of pretzel-like embraces, copulating like crazed octopi. Sitting up, upside down, ankles behind the head, every which way. All of which might have been less outrageous had not the genitalia been so clearly and meticulously articulated. There was absolutely no ambiguity about what was being depicted in the panels of the vase. The precision and detail of the artist's pen was remarkable in its exactitude. The men had mad priapic eyes, pointy beards, and extraordinarily long, thin penises that curved upwards like scimitars.

Dazed, like a boxer pummeled across a ring, he sought refuge in the more innocuous parts of the vase, in the harmless decoration of the panels, and down in the flowers. But he was slapped back by these too. *My god, even here.* Even between the oval portrait panels, in the paisley background that he had thought to be a profusion of flora, he now saw that the paisleys were actually hundreds—if not thousands—of disembodied breasts, each like the petal of a flower, but each also clearly taking the shape of a breast complete with a nipple and aureole.

On the bottom of the vase, on a white sticker, was printed:

KAMA SUTRA

17

INDIA

After another spell of staring, after taking in the full measure of his folly, he placed the jug back into its box. He closed his eyes and leaned his head back against the sign pole, breathing deeply. He remained still for fifteen seconds. Then, his eyes still closed, he rolled his head from side to side; he beat out, slowly but emphatically, sixteen gongs with his head, each one resounding up and down the pole like a funeral bell.

I, am, so, stupid.
I, am, so, stupid.
I, am, so, stupid.
I, am, so, stupid.

29

He did not sleep that night—could not sleep that night—except for a few blurred, exhausted, burnt-out minutes near the end of the night, when the blue had already begun to seep in through the slats of his blinds, and the city was beginning to stir awake. The cracked jug, like the crooked leer of a dirty old man in Pigeon Alley, mocked him from even inside its hidden box, tucked away under a heap of clothes in the bottom of his closet.

He lay with his eyes clamped shut, burning and dry like chunks of pumice, eggs of stone; his innards fed on the darkness and the broken flesh of his thoughts; his mind was dense with bundled shouting thorns.

She was his happiness and he would never have her. Never. He had always known that—that he would never have her—but still he had hoped, foolishly, pointlessly, squandering rivers of thought, kingdoms of hours. He had built palaces and enshrined her as his queen; in white silk slippers, she glided across the expansive, polished teak floors; a sunbeam illuminated a spray of salmon roses in a blue vase.

No one would ever want him. Not her, not anyone. And even if he did find someone—someone, someday— he would always crave her, he would always see her beyond the transparency of the moment, the ghost behind his eyes, his hours, a shifting gleam behind a curtain, her skin—he would always dream of what it would have been like to have her, to have had a life with her, to have felt her hand on his stomach in the close night.

Eugene believed, with the conviction of all those who have been a long time in the hole, that he would never be happy again. He was as convinced of the permanence and immutability of his unhappiness as firmly and unshakably as others—as a prophet, perhaps, in the full throes of revelation—might be convinced of a wheel of fire in the sky or an I and Thou dialogue with the Divine. All his webs of reference, all his strands of logic, all the arteries of thought—all the force of every argument and every interpretation of the world—from a gust of wind, to the granite sierras thrusting up from the body of the earth— pointed irrevocably and irrefutably to the one final proof that he would never again be happy, that the long drought of despair would never be broken, that it would have dominion forever.

30

It seemed only a few moments later that he was awakened by the noise of his family at breakfast: clinking spoons and whistling teapots, and his grandmother's television vibrating on the kitchen counter. Eugene wrapped his head in the pillow, trying to muffle the din of the morning.

A half-hour later, still dizzy and dry-eyed from lack of sleep, he was shuffling off to his uncle's deli, his cheerless step falling in with the Monday morning march of the countless thousands who were also on their way to work, trudging to jobs that they hated but endured in order to pay the rent, the car insurance, the impossibly high tuition for college.

Eugene had a gloomy intuition that this was going to be his life: an inglorious irritated march to the grave, jostled along in the maddening mob, competing, struggling, attaining nothing. Bringing a couple kids into the world so that they could repeat the same misfortunes and miseries in the next generation. Where was the meaning in any of it?

Eugene mulled over these things, murkily, his head down, swept westward with the morose thousands, the glum and beaten hordes: the lot of them were like cattle shambling up the ramps to the slaughterhouse, sniffing blood and death, helpless, defeated, almost welcoming the falling knife. Ahead of Eugene lay the remainder of high school, with its APs and SATs, cram schools and clubs, volunteer work and all the other impossible demands made by colleges—all those schools with ivy walls and marble columns, sanctums of exclusion and prestige, none of which would be impressed by Eugene, with his 87 average, skinny chest and clumsy tongue that would fail to function were he ever fool enough to request an interview.

31

The days passed dully as he tried to forget her, to put his whole doomed longing to rest. At work, whenever he could, he avoided all customers and left the register to his uncle, preferring to be left alone to rotate and restock the fruits and vegetables. The fruits, even in full sun, seemed drained and pale, the memory of a photograph.

His eyes were dry and he was always thirsty. He didn't eat much, just a banana now and then, and spent his short lunch break in the shady grassless park off Parsons Boulevard, near Bowne House, where the homeless slept on benches and old people sat alone. Eugene sat wherever there was a vacant bench, his head in his hands, raising his eyes occasionally to watch the pigeons digging in their feathers for fleas. One time, he dimly perceived that one of the pigeons was missing a foot, that it had just a little nub of red above the ankle. He put his head back down, and in the following days, he did not see the bird again.

At home, he stayed in his room, in the dark, staring up at a swirl of despair. He didn't even go out walking. He didn't want to walk all the way to the water, to look out over the bay to the twinkling lights on the other shore. He would have to find some other place to walk.

32

On one of his sunken evenings, Eugene was lying in bed, headphones on his ears, listening to nothing. Just the murmuring chorus of his unhappy thoughts, voices at a wake. The disk had ended a while ago and he had little interest in playing it again. He could hear, muted by the headphones and the door, the sizzling staccato of the television and the many-layered hum of air conditioners up and down the block laying down hymns into the canyons of brick below.

There was a gentle knock on his door, and it was his sister, holding a plate of sliced pineapple. She entered quietly.

"I thought you might like these," she said, and placed it down on the table by the bed.

He looked at the plate for a few long moments. It was blue, and the pineapples were sliced into plump triangles, the way his mother would cut them. A small silver fork lay at the edge of the plate.

He felt the back of his throat getting a little sore.

"Thank you," he managed to say, and turned away.

33

The next morning, on his way to work, Eugene passed a dumpster, one piled high with black bags and broken furniture, one that nearly made him vomit from the sudden violence of its stink. He hurried on, trying not to breathe, stepping over a trickle of foul milky ooze that leaked from the dumpster and snaked across the sidewalk to the gutter. The heat of the morning closed in around him, prickly and damp; the silvery haze of the sky promised that the day would be a scorcher.

Some fifty yards ahead, against a wall, a homeless man was slumped amidst his kingdom of rags and bottles. The morning crowds streamed past him and his hopelessly proffered cup, paying him no more mind than they would a fire hydrant or garbage can. Seeing the man, Eugene nodded to himself, chastened by an inchoate and humbling thought: Now there was a man who had it rough: outside in all weathers—sunbaked in summer and freezing in winter, soaking wet in the rains—chased away by supers, harassed by cops, tormented by idle and vicious teens.

Driven mad by shame and the crushing emptiness of his days, by the exhausting grind of hunger and thirst and broken sleep. Tortured by a mind that had turned in on itself; that had become locked into whatever cycle of urgency, whatever torrent of wasted thought that years ago had sucked him down into the dirty foamy hole where he would forever spin, but never quite drown, like a cork churning and bobbing in a storm sewer.

Life goes on for this man whether he wants it or not. In the long razor night, he is snagged from harassing dreams by car horns, dog barks, sudden shouting. He tenses and listens, judging the danger (how many are they—kids?

Dogs? Gasoline?); he reaches for his weapon, a screw-driver with a chipped handle—and then settles back into his uneasy haunted ground between sleeping and waking, turning over on the concrete or drafty grate, easing the pains in his hip and shoulder.

When the next day comes, bleakly, another day of hardpan and bleached bones, he is not thinking what Eugene is thinking—about high school and college, or the sweet pain of Soo Yun—no, the issues of a homeless man are much more urgent than that: he is thinking, in his cardboard box agony, *how will I get through the next twenty minutes?*

"Spare some change, help me out?"

Eugene had been passing by the homeless man without looking at him.

"Come on, man, I'm *hungry!*"

The spike in the man's voice, the complaint, made Eugene turn. The man was glaring up at Eugene indignantly, even defiantly. One of his eyes was glazed over with a cataract. After a few seconds, seeing that Eugene had stopped, the man softened his tone.

"All I want to do," he said, "is get something to eat." He rocked forward, lifting his cup. His other hand cradled a blackened foot, cracked with calluses and broken toenails.

"If you could help me," he added, "I'd appreciate it."

Eugene remained standing in front of the man, looking at him, startled by the clarity and correctness of the man's plea: the man *was* hungry. Eugene *could* help him out. It really was that simple. A clear human equation. Eugene dug into his pants pocket and scooped out a fistful of small change—nickels and dimes, a quarter or two, even pennies—that he had emptied from his change jar that morning, a type of hungry gleaning he had not had to do in a long time. The eighty dollars had wiped him out. He had a weighty fistful of coins, three dollars and thirty cents, enough for two slices of pizza, and he was about to pick through the change when he suddenly thought: to hell with it, give him all of it, he needs it more than I do. Eugene dropped the whole jingling mass of coins into the man's cup.

The cup dipped sharply, and the man looked up.

"Thanks, man," he said. "You're all right."

He held out his hand for Eugene to shake, and Eugene shook it, feeling the hard tacky skin.

"God bless you," said the man. "And I mean that, too. I ain't just saying that."

"You too," said Eugene, and continued on his way, resisting the impulse to wipe his palm on his pants. His stomach relaxed, and when he raised his eyes to look ahead, a little color burst through the day to tint the trees and shops with red and gold and green.

34

L ater that day, as he sorted through the clusters of grapes, shooing off the bees and picking off the ones that had gone soft, mushy at the top, it occurred to him that just as all these fruits and vegetables would be gone within a week—bought, eaten, or tossed out to rot in a hot, fly-buzzing landfill—so would be gone all these people bustling down Roosevelt Avenue with shopping bags, new shoes, or their hair just done up perfectly for forty dollars. All these people would disappear in what: sixty, seventy years? The old people would be gone after a few more winters; his parents' generation would fade away in another forty; Eugene himself would be dead and gone in what—fifty years? Sixty? Maybe less, maybe tomorrow—hit by a fruit truck.

He dropped a handful of grapes into the garbage and then surprised himself with a small laugh, a sudden snort through the nose, his first bit of mirth in days. Some relief: in the end, nothing really mattered. With a kind of serene amusement, he looked out on the sidewalk: even all these girls, giddy in the bloom of their first sweet beauty, giggling into cellphones and walking arm in arm; squeezing into photobooths for smiling sticker pictures—they were all gone, they were all dead. Just an inch below their glowing skin were skeletons, the same frames of bones as were in the middle aged and the old, the same as were in the old bent women who struggled up the block, their backs hooked like candy canes and their knotted hands gripping bags of groceries, unable to see farther than a foot or two up the gum-stained sidewalk. After picking up some eggs and crackers, they retraced their steps back to their hot rented rooms, returning like old geese on their last migrations, dying on the shores of some black lake, their feathers dragging in the mud, hanging onto life long after there seemed to be any joy or point in living.

Everywhere Eugene looked, he saw skeletons. Up and down the avenue, grinning skulls jabbered at each other, getting their ghoulish witches' hair groomed and glossed for the graveyard; they tilted back in salon chairs, combed and coddled by other chattering skulls, gossiping idly about handbags, husbands, or a new line of perfumes they had seen advertised on the side of a bus. All vanity and chasing of wind. Outside, on the street, sharp skulls clicked by in silk suits and Italian shoes, their cleft chins clinching deals into flip phones, each breezy rack of ribs a ladder of ambition. The whole parade was absurd, ghastly—a pageant of the pompous ephemeral—the hollow knocking of bones in the graveyard.

As he watched life and death pulse by him on the street, a stroboscopic blinking of flesh, then bones, flesh, then bones, Eugene felt lightened by a strange sense of calm, by the spirit of grace. He went on sorting through the fruits, feeling like an archangel on judgment day, sorting through the saints and sinners, saving some but dropping others into the blackened pit of the wastebasket, where they would moulder away into nothing.

As he worked, his arms and fingers falling into a trancelike rhythm, it amused him to see the bones and tendons of his own hands shifting beneath the surface of the skin, their architecture so plainly visible. With a kind of wordless pity, he was touched by the desire of the flesh to remain vital, to so stridently insist on its own immortality when the juries of time were so clearly against it; to keep up its futile, self-clutching clamor as had the thousands of human generations before him, as had innumerable birds shivering in the cold of a million winters, as was—even now, on the delicatessen floor—this small ant scrambling from beneath the shadow of Eugene's foot, trying to save its brief, tiny life, impelled by the instinct that has driven all evolution.

He felt on the threshold of a revelation, on the verge of hearing, rising above the dull rumble of the street—the sweet sad music of humanity, the song of life and death weaving its colors and rhythms around the void like the twisting helices of a strand of DNA. He was on the verge of hearing all this, of understanding all and renouncing all, of casting off—as had his grandmother's Buddha, or Saint Francis, or any mendicant monk—of casting off the husk of his desire-riven self to pierce through to the unencumbered heart of the world, where all things—the birds, the lambs, even the beams of sunlight—spoke with the same pure eloquence.

He was on the verge of such transcendence, that is—such serene vaulting into the timeless hereafter—until Soo Yun passed by on the street outside, until Soo Yun passed by in the gap of the sun flaps, until the sight of her snapped him back *into the now* like a baby slapped at birth. He inhaled sharply, the gasp of one startled from a dream, and he watched helplessly as she—the late afternoon light bringing out the auburn of her hair—stepped lightly across the narrow slit of his vision and disappeared. His crystal nirvana was shattered, his meditative calm: paradise lost, samsara regained. His angelic choirs fell apart, their singing devolving into discord beneath the noise and clatter of the day; and on the street, the girls, joyously enfleshed, skeletons no more, bounced by in their full ripeness.

35

T wo days later at four o'clock, when the sky was just beginning to rumble with thunder, she came in. It was the twenty-third of August, a full week and a half since Queens Day, and he had begun to wonder whether he would ever see her again. He feared that the brief glimpse of her through the slit might be all he would get. She might have gone off to college already, in a car crammed with books, clothes and computer equipment; the car would be driven by her father, dignified and silent, dutifully pressing down the indicator long before he changed lanes; and in the front seat beside him was Soo Yun's mother, proud and anxious, awed by her daughter's achievement yet unprepared for the void that Soo Yun's graduation would leave in her life (no more driving her to violin lessons, or Julliard, or Joyce Academy for SATs). Soo Yun might have already settled into her new life at Princeton, making friends, leaning back on one arm and laughing under trees, or attracting long hungry gazes as she sailed across campus in her sundress.

In the two days since he had last seen her, when his visions of eternity had vanished and flesh had become flesh again, he'd thoroughly planned what he wanted to say to her, rehearsing it in his head while at work and then aloud over the evening streets home. He gestured like an actor, sculpting every word and phrase, and dropping his voice to a murmur whenever passing someone with a dog.

He had planned it all out, but when she appeared suddenly that afternoon, stepping in off the darkening sidewalk and ducking her head under the sun flaps, he found himself—as he always did when suddenly confronted with her—incapable of even the most minimal functioning.

As he stood at the register, a mute mannequin, she picked out two plums and placed them on the aluminum tray of the scale. As she was busy with her purse, snapping open the clasp and poking for change, he stared at her, his mouth partly open, a deep-water fish. The sounds of the street seemed far away, swirling whirls of distant sound, as if they had been sucked down into the bottom of a shell, where they were awaiting the pressing of an expectant ear to be heard at all.

By an extreme force of will, he managed to rip his gaze from her and punch numbers into the electronic scale.

"How much is it?" she asked, looking up. She glanced at the scale and smiled. "That can't be right."

With another effort, he looked at the glowing red numbers on the scale. They read $79.49. He had charged her $99.99 per pound.

"No, that's not right," he agreed, his voice a rupture. He coughed into his hand. "That should be 99 cents a pound." He punched in the correct rate and the new price was 80 cents.

"That's more like it," she smiled, and gave him a dollar.

He scooped two dimes out of the register and held them out to her opened hand. His nails brushed her palms as he let go of the coins. He had not felt any of her skin with his fingertips. It had all been nail.

"Thank you," she said and reached for the plums, her whole body already shifted towards the street.

"Your bag," he said.

She was momentarily confused. She had her bag. He had meant a paper bag for the plums, and held up the smallest size.

"Oh, that's okay," she said. "I'm going to eat them now. I'll take a napkin, though."

He smiled magnanimously.

"I'll give you a napkin," he said. "And a bag. You deserve only the best."

She laughed and yielded the plums to him. "Okay, if you insist."

He was pleased with the way things were going. He was warming up. The clot in his throat was gone and he was appearing to be, amazingly, stepping into the role of the smooth young cashier that he had always imagined for himself. He bagged the plums, inserted a napkin, and folded the bag into a tidy package. He then presented it to her with a flourish.

"Here you go."

"Thank you," she said.

"No problem," he said. And then, urging himself on, not wanting to lose momentum: "By the way, how was Korea?"

She looked at him strangely.

"How did you know I went to Korea?"

He knew he looked surprised, but there was nothing he could do. She obviously hadn't remembered. As he tried to mask his hurt, he was acutely aware of the two other women waiting in line, shifting their weight impatiently, but he didn't care. It was too late to stop now.

"You told me," he said, with an almost despairing honesty, but then, realizing he might have caused her some embarrassment: "Not that you should even remember, of course. It was way back in July, around the time of ... well, it was back in July."

She shut her purse and shook her head, as if gently chiding herself for the lapse of memory. Then she suddenly brightened.

"Oh, I remember now," she said. "I remember telling you. It was the day of a thunderstorm." She collected her bag from the counter. "Okay, take care now."

She started to walk out of the store. The flash of her white shorts was the last thing he saw before the green sun flaps closed behind her.

His thoughts surged, tumbling over themselves. *Thunderstorm?* There had been no thunderstorm the day he had asked her to Queens Day, he was convinced of it. He had memorized that entire brittle conversation (that entire day, for that matter), and had burned it permanently into his synapses—there had been no storm that day. It had been a hot gray day that cast no shadows, he was sure of it. Thunderstorms, he knew about thunderstorms: she had never run wet and dripping into his store.

The next woman in line, a small old lady with an umbrella, placed a bunch of bananas on the scale and he reflexively punched in the price. Then a rushing thought: what if she had been thinking of him during those thunderstorms the same way that he had been thinking about her? What if she had felt some of the same electricity? What if she had felt, beneath the bruised and rumbling sky, some of the urgency of his love, the voltage of his passion, carried to her through the damp and supercharged air—he imagined a spasm of lightning arcing through a cloud. It was possible, right? Why else would she have linked him with a storm?

He bounded out from behind the counter, rushing past the old woman as she vigorously blinked her eyes, shaking a bag of grapes at him. He didn't care. He ran past the orange and lemon bins, past the ice barrel with the ready-cut fruits. He slapped aside the plastic sunshade and exploded out onto the sidewalk, making a kid with earphones jump back, startled ("What the—?").

Soo Yun was about a hundred feet down the sidewalk, walking quickly for a bus, almost breaking into a trot. Above the shops all down Roosevelt, surging clouds of luminous, electric gray tumbled eastward, the front of a storm. A damp gust of wind blew dust in Eugene's eyes.

"Soo Yun!" he cried. "Soo Yun!"

On his second call, she turned, and seeing him coming, she hesitated, looking from him to the bus.

He ran up to her.

"Soo Yun," he said. "I'm sorry. It's about the festival, Queens Day." His words were tumbling out and there was nothing he could do to stop them.

"It's about the festival, the one I invited you to. I just wanted to tell you that I wasn't able to go there, at least not until it was almost closed. I only had about five minutes there and I didn't have enough time to get you anything good, like I said I would. I'm sorry."

She was looking at him thoughtfully, first with a kind of confused alarm but then with sympathetic indulgence, as if she had been wondering whether she should be wary of this boy who had just chased her down the street, this boy who worked at the fruit store, but then decided that no, he was nothing to worry about—he was just a high school kid, a good kid, a boy who worked at his family's store and went to school with her little brother.

"I'm sorry," he said again. "I promised to get you something but I didn't."

"That's all right," she said gently. "It's okay, it doesn't matter."

A boom of thunder over by the airport.

"But it does matter," said Eugene. "It does."

She was looking at him carefully. He was afraid she might laugh and more than anything, he did not want her to laugh.

She reached out and touched his forearm softly.

"Thank you," she said. "Thank you for thinking of me. That was very sweet of you."

He looked down, somewhere between her feet and his. A few drops of rain had begun to fall, leaving big dark splotches the size of quarters on the sidewalk.

"Look," she said, quietly. "I have to go. I'd like to catch that bus before the rain comes. Is that okay?"

He nodded, and then looked at her and at the bus. The wind was picking up and was starting to snap the streamers in front of the stores. Umbrellas were popping open up and down the avenue and people were running for buses, the subway, and shops.

"Okay?" she asked. Her voice was still quiet.

Eugene nodded. "Okay."

She turned and started off down the block, and as the drops came harder, she broke into a little trot and held the bag of plums over her head like a tiny umbrella. She fell in with the other women who were running for the bus with short choppy steps, and then the crowd closed behind her, swallowing her from his sight.

36

He stood for a moment, calmly, looking after her and hearing nothing but his breathing. People crossed in front of him, both ways, hurrying, hopping up onto the curb from the gusty street of headlights. Some appeared to be talking, calling to each other—their mouths were moving—but Eugene couldn't hear them: they were silent reflections passing over glass.

She was gone, that was it. A flick of the tail and she was off into the river of life, gone in the current. And even if he were to see her again, it wouldn't matter, it wouldn't help him—it wouldn't ease his longing. The ache of an old wound, a broken bone that had never healed.

Then, a sizzling crack, a flash, and thunder shook the avenue, sending great cannonades booming eastward up Roosevelt towards Union Street, shaking windows and rattling doors, setting off car alarms and dog barks. Then came the rain, in a huge rush after a moment of stillness, as powerful and soaking a deluge as any that had come down all summer.

Eugene stood a while on the sidewalk, the drops erupting around his feet in splashing silver sparkles. He remained standing, not moving, the only person in all of

Queens not ducking for cover, not running into a building or a bus or a bank; he stood feeling the warm rain drumming down upon his head and neck and shoulders; it ran in rivulets off his hair and down his forehead and into his eyes.

It was pouring down on the street and sidewalks and cars and buses, falling so hard that the windshield wipers—on high—strained to push up the weight of the water, bending like the poles of vaulters pushing away from the earth. Through the crescent curves on the windows emerged—and then were bleared again—the pale faces of drivers, heads forward over the wheel, straining to see through the glass.

It was raining on the awning of his uncle's store, bellying the green canvas; it was splashing down silver and slapping, in surging streams, a few inches from the pineapples, the peaches, and the plums; it streamed down on the upended bean bushel that Pasquale had left out beyond the flaps, its yellow wood soaking to brown, the stool he used when sorting through the string beans, snapping off the dried and withered ends, tossing out the moldy ones, *pensando de su esposa y niños en* Ecuador, Quito, imagining them in his half-finished cinderblock house atop a hilltop ridge, its rough gray walls painted with the red letters *Se Vende*.

107

It was raining on Bowne house, and its pigeons, and on the narrow strip of park where he used to sit, steeped in sadness, among the old people.

It was also raining on Flushing Creek, on its garbage-choked reeds, its half sunk orange pylons, its rusted shopping carts; it was coming down on the subway trestle over the creek, on its oil-brown ties and silver ribbons of track shivering west past the stadium, to Corona, Jackson Heights, and Woodside; it was raining on the red shells of the 7 train, with their wet gray linoleum floors dirtied with footprints, soggy papers, and empty coffee cups that described half-circles on the floor as they rolled with the motion of the train; and in the front of the train, looking out the rain-streaked window, stands a boy with his feet apart and his forehead resting against the glass, his head making the same rolling motion on the glass as the coffee cup is making on the floor.

It was also raining on Douglaston Bay, and Bayside Marina, which was bare now except for some buckets of pink water and rods leaning up against the rails, their lines still out in the water. It was raining across the bay, too, on the dark leaves of Douglaston, the leaves shining and shaking in the rain; also on the houses in which he had envisioned her, her head tilted back, ice cubes tinkling like sacred music.

It was raining on Flushing Meadows Park and its giant globe, and on the parade grounds where the festival had been held, on the grass that was recovering its spring, on the fields wriggling with worms flushed from their holes. It was raining on the wide elm under which Eugene had bought his jug, and also on the Mobil station where he had unwrapped it, and had dropped it; in the puddles of the gas station rainbows gathered, iridescent paisleys of gasoline afloat on the water, the puddles creeping amoeba-like across the concrete expanse of the station, drawn by gravity, a Tao of movement.

And in Manhattan, down by the Battery, on the harbor, it was raining on the ferry, and it was also raining on Stuyvesant High School, from which Soo Yun had graduated, in a gown, holding a scroll; it was drumming on the lumpy roof of Eugene's school, popping on the aluminum vents and ducts from where he would graduate next year, after one more revolution of the planet around the sun, and then he would head off to college, to states unknown.

A few blocks away, it was raining on the homeless man with his creased and wrinkled cup, with his black scabs and cracked soles, his broken yellowed toenails; it was raining all over Flushing, all over Queens, on garbage dumps and gardens, junk yards and cemeteries, gracious, unstinting, prodigal.

And then something gave way within him, some hard shell yielding to the moist warmth of germination, something in the deep and the dark of the loam—the impulse that drives the flower, the groaning of the stem towards the light.

It was acceptable that he would never have her: she had enlarged his soul, illuminated it. She had perhaps enriched it more by his doomed and earnest longing than she might have had she been his as he had so ardently wanted her to be. He'd been awakened to the wild and barren places of the heart: crevices crammed with seed; roots that seek the water, stems that seek the light; it was through her that he'd felt the great granite shoulders of the world thrust up through his darkness and carry him up with it.

Pasquale called to him. He was standing beneath the awning, laughing and waving for him to come back. All around him, the oranges and lemons were illuminated like an island of stained glass on the darkened street. His uncle was standing there, too, with his arms crossed, near some girls with their hair wet and black and hanging down over their shoulders. The day was dark and dense, and as the drops of rain fell past the awning, past the bright silver verge, falling downward, downward, like sheets of beads, it seemed as if the whole store, gold and luminous, with its embedded jewels of fruit, was rising into the air like an offering.

TED CLEARY

TED CLEARY

AFTERWORD

GERMINAL

N ow that the show is over and most people have left the theater, and the ushers, having loosened their ties, are now reaching for their brooms, perhaps the few playgoers who've lingered to chat or stretch won't mind a brief tour backstage.

This novella has its own origin story, which some readers have asked about, and so at the small risk of treading on some orthodoxies—but not, thank God, risking electrocution—I'll put it here, hidden away in a slim afterword where only the most dogged readers will sniff it out. Everyone else can safely and serenely ignore it.

To paraphrase E.N. Nospone, an early champion of jazz LP liner notes, it's perhaps better to keep story and backstory warm between the same covers than to frigidly chaperone them into separate beds and sheets. Nonetheless, with a respectful nod to New Criticism, I won't venture more than a baby's toenail into *interpretation,* which properly remains the playground and province of the reader. And the story naturally stands on its own.

So, the background: this novella arose quite by chance out of teaching in Queens, NYC. Although downtown Flushing has no "Joyce Academy" *(un huevo de Pascua),* there are dozens of little "academies" in Queens, Brooklyn, Jersey and elsewhere dedicated to after-school study, enrichment, and test prep. For many years, I taught at one of the first and longest-lasting of the Flushing schools, owned by an entrepreneurial Korean family, the Kwons, and it was a refreshing, no b.s. place to work: hard-working students and families; zero bureaucracy, no pretensions or politics (and if there were politics, I wasn't aware of them); and the one and only job requirement was *to be good*—if you were good, you could stay for decades; if you weren't, you were gone by lunch: *annyeonghi gaseyo* (안녕히 가세요) and have a nice day.

The school was right there amidst all the crowds, noise, grit, and fumes; amidst all the pedestrians and peddlers, shops and street-sellers; among the many incoming buses and trains. It was also just around the corner from what I imagined to be Eugene's deli—an actual deli, but with no Eugene. This vibrant hub became the setting for the story.

In writing classes I taught fundamentals—content, structure, and style—and in reading classes we drilled down into the material until we hit something alive. Exploring beyond the routine practice questions, we surveyed literature and history, decoded the rhetorical strategies of passages, and unearthed the etymologies of key words. There's great subversive illumination in the merry excavation of, say, "prestige" [*etym.* "trickery, deceit"] in a milieu where "Harvard" has the mythic resonance of "Heaven." Roots, truth, epiphany, humor—and humor wears no foolish face of praise.

Each year in the rotating readings would bubble up a passage from James Joyce's "Araby" (the market-chalice sequence), followed by a few dull and plodding reading comp questions (O the barbarity! … but at least the kids got a little green-shoot nibble of Joyce); despite the somewhat herbicidal context of test prep, the students responded to the language and to the lush theme of infatuation (they were of the age); and every year, in the somewhat forlorn and quixotic hope of getting youth interested in literature, I'd ask, *Think for a second: is the boy's adventure in old Dublin really so different from your own experiences right now?* and then improvise a transposed riff from Joyce's Irish market to the contemporary Asian bustle right outside the door (now my Ch. 6); the students immediately got it: flickers of recognition, a bit of a pulse, a quickening of life; then I'd wrap by giving them a copy of "Araby" and suggesting, *OK now, so why don't you let it rip and write the whole story, reinvent it, make it new… this is everybody's story now.*

Every year this scene was repeated, and every year (surprise) none of the kids wrote a thing. Each year, though, I was reminded of the idea, of the aptness and fertility of it—and the lingering allure of transplanting the premise continually put out roots; and finally, since the attraction would not go away—and since I was starting to feel what can only be called *a debt to the gods*—I surrendered to the dunning and started writing it myself.

I let it free to grow wherever it wanted, to run wild like a bunch of kids at play in a field, and after about three years of enchantment, during which it never really left my mind, I finished it. The story had its own legs and spirit, and I just followed its scent and tracks through the underbrush. Organic inductive process—you know the deal.

Song of the Cicada expanded well beyond "Araby" (about 10x longer), even after I pulled it back from other wayward directions. It ended in the right place. Any more would have been too much. And just translating "Araby" stroke for stroke would have been a cute exercise but little more. In wanting to be itself, the story summoned the street symphonies and the sister and the whole coda of the vase and the rain and all the other sultry textural detail. The Irish acorn became an American oak. But the boy's agonized longing remains by far the dominant theme—as it should be.

It's fair to say that the story contains not only a nod and homage to the grandmaster Joyce but also to New York, which has long been an immigrant city, a destination for millions seeking more flourishing lives: Irish and Italians and Jews and Latinos and Africans and Asians—and while the streets aren't paved with gold for Eugene (they're paved with black gum spots...), they abound with a living fullness of which he's becoming more aware (thanks

119

in part to Soo Yun); and so the theme of organic growth shoots up through this Queens tale more than through Joyce's iconic tales of paralysis and suffocation ("Eveline," "Counterparts," "A Little Cloud," "A Painful Case"). The Ireland of a hundred years ago was a more stifled and strangled place than Queens is today.

Two examples, close to home: my father's parents—Kerry fishermen farmers—having fought one war, emigrated in 1922 during the Irish civil war ("It's one thing to fight the Brits, another to fight your cousins"); and my mother left in the 1950s— no opportunity: another Irish teenager made for export. Though O'Donovan Rossa's native land had its many unmatched glories (and music and stories), *You can't eat the scenery,* as they ruefully say, and up through the 1950s, the island was also a bit of a poor and provincial backwater; some say it slowly killed the likes of Flann O'Brien—who, unlike Joyce, never got out. There's plenty of Ireland in the story, and also of Asian Queens, and many of the other flavors that spice up the line along the purple 7 train to *last stop no passengers Flushing Main Street.*

Given its main theme of infatuation, the novella is inevitably kind of sexy (and definitely sensual and sensory)—but also, especially given the wretched excess of our anything-goes Kaliyuga age—remarkably chaste. The nervous should note that the only explicitly sexual imagery comes via the Indian Kama Sutra vase, a shocking and hilarious rupture—since one might see it as Eugene's discretion exploding and spewing out what he can't really acknowledge. The gnomon, the iceberg, the zeppole.

Despite its *picante* zest, the language of that well-wrought urn is completely valid (our chef says no substitute wasabi for the hotter words—*it is what it is:* no budging, arms crossed, hissing steam and pot-clang); so ahead of any lace-curtain fluster and bluster, I can only shrug and say: *Hey, it's the Kama Sutra, classical Indian art and literature going back to the 3rd century, so please take up any objections with the great Hindu masters.* Peace and goodness abound.

Thanks for your time and generous attention, and I hope to see you next time around.

Ted Cleary
New York City

ABOUT THE AUTHOR

T ed Cleary is a writer and artist from New York City. He received degrees in Law and English & Comparative Literature from Columbia University, where he was also awarded fellowships and creative writing prizes. Authors studied closely included Joyce, Nabokov, Swift, and Flann O' Brien. Along with teaching English literature and writing in and around New York, he has served as an assistant district attorney.

Several city tales continue to be collected into "New York Stories," and a number of travel experiences have been gathered into essays. While living in Harlem, he translated *Rebobinando +1*, a book of Spanish poems by Patricia Fernández-Pacheco.

Apropos of Eugene's shop in *Song of the Cicada,* in his student years, the author worked as a fruit and vegetable seller on the Bronx—Yonkers city line, right across from the numberless summer cicadas of Van Cortlandt Park.

OTHER TITLES

AT THE END OF THE WORLD

A FRACTAL META LOCO NARRATIVE IN E-FLAT MAJOR

"If Hieronymus Bosch came back to write a novella, it might look like this." – *The Phoenix*

"This is intensely good writing, overflowing with raw artistry." – James Howard Kunstler, *Young Man Blues*

A psychedelic and picaresque romp through philosophy, jazz, and a plausible end-of-the-world scenario, this tight novella spins interwoven story-lines, draws you down corkscrewing rabbit holes, lifts you back to open air—and finally catapults you (along with "Dean the saxophone player") into realms strangely alluring and unknown.

Greatly compressed, this packs the punch of an entire novel into the M-80 cylinder of a short novella. For readers lacking time (and that's all of us), this quick in-and-out literary head-trip may be just the thing.

Excerpt: Along with the monks of San Sebastián and a few dismal souls whose aesthetic included the bruise-purple beauties of suicide, Dean, the saxophone player, was looking for-ward to the end of the world. This anticipation, however, derived from no morbid fasc-ination: it arose from the impetus it would give his art.

He was a musician who performed most brilliantly in contexts where sanity and tonality seemed in the gravest danger of extinction. Several years earlier, he had been the leader of the Creedmoor Quartet, a group of five jazz players with histories of demonic possession. Although their number was five, they refused to acknowledge this in their name for fear of attracting the pentangular forces of Satan.

Dean relished sessions with these players, their techniques perfect but their ideas diabolical—several leagues beyond bizarre by even the most esoteric standards—the tonal center of their pieces forever spinning off into disparate and incongruous corners of the musical sound garden. While the madmen ran wild like panicked horses, bastards of tonality, Dean gave chase and circled them, darting, dodging, dropping notes at their feet, framing harmonic shims for their manic micro-tones and half steps.

To some degree perhaps, Dean's balancing role had been foreordained, had been tapped into the spinning rims of fate by his having been born a leap-year child, a baby slapped alive on the 29th day of the shortest month, on that little shimmy of sunlight wedged into the winter quadrennial—to keep true the Gregorian cycle, to keep the wheels of time from wobbling overmuch on its pitted road through the human mind. And on this day, the last day, he was looking to shore up more than music or calendars: he was shoring up the whole collapsing world.

"Hats off—just right for our apocalyptic age. Reminds me of early Pynchon in a very good way—terrific—such economical writing with constant dashes of rhetorical brilliance." — Eumaeus Jones, Ph.D.

"I enjoyed *At the End of the World* immensely. Seriously beautiful writing. It's been a long, long time since I've read anyone who demonstrates such a love for the richness of language and for solid historical references, and who can do so without sounding or being the least bit pretentious ... the obvious love for other, non-English vocabularies is also immediately attractive."
— T. Harrington, Prof. of Iberian Studies, Trinity College

"Rarely has the sign-off for *The End* resonated so blissfully in secular fiction." — Michael Seidel, Prof. of English & Comparative Literature, Columbia University

TED CLEARY

TEENAGE WILDLIFE: DAVID BOWIE

Less a biography of the iconic rock star (1947-2016) than an exploration of a listener's early immersion in the music, this idiosyncratic essay teases out—and weaves back together—diverse strands of Bowie's songs and persona, the author's 1980's Bronx Irish-Italian culture, and riffing associative meditations on art and immortality. There's energy here, and color and spark, but the center holds, just as Bowie's songs adhered to classic form even amidst their flash and strut of Ziggy Stardust.

Composed immediately following Bowie's death in Jan 2016, and touched up lightly later, "Teenage Wildlife" is both a homage to an audacious artist and a rediscovery of those islands of memory that exist, at times half-forgotten, in every listener's experience.

SNAPSHOTS OF BELARUS: MINSK

Chronicling a train journey from Moscow to Minsk, in a backdoor quest to get a friend's Russian visa renewed, this short travelogue pairs scrupulous

126

observation with occasional Gogolian turns, in keeping with the spirit of the former Soviet bloc.

Excerpt: A little later, in the vastly empty park of the white memorial, an old woman entered, hobbling slightly, and sat down at a nearby bench. I nodded to her, but she did not appear to see me. She was bundled in a brown ochre coat with her stockings rolled up just past the knee. She appeared to be in her late sixties or seventies—which would have made her a little girl during the war—but appearances can deceive here in Belarus, and in Russia, where people—and just about everything else—weather quickly from the long cheerless winters.

She opened her bag and took out a box of cigarettes, its logo a pale blue disc encircling a black bull's eye. She lit a cigarette, turning away from the wind and hunching slightly to protect the flame. She carefully placed the spent match on the bench and then leaned back to relish her smoke. And relish it she did, for hers was not a casual smoke: it was a serious and mindful smoke—a scrupulously intense, closed-eyed drafting deep into her lungs (and then retaining it there for several seconds) as if she were aspirating the very fumes of paradise.

When she inhaled, she cocked her head slightly towards the sun, a heliotropic plant, and puckered her lips to drag fiercely at the butt. Her cheeks crumpled from the strain, and the wrinkles of her mouth aligned tightly like the grooves and folds of a paper umbrella.

She sucked with such vigor that it seemed the cigarette were smoking her instead of she the cigarette, and then suddenly she flew up—head, body, boots and all—and disappeared into the butt of the smoke, sucked like a doll into a vacuum cleaner.

The cigarette then flipped upward, end over end, a sparkling pinwheel, and finally landed with a surprised shock on the footpath, where it was scrutinized briefly by red-toed pigeons with abruptly swiveling heads.

A DINGLE SONATA

Several pieces revolving around the Irish town of Dingle in West Kerry, including *Curly Wee & Gussie Goose,* about the 1940s childhood of the author's mother; a found letter from a man who emigrated "to survive"—psychologically more than physically; and "Relations," a story from the Irish diaspora in Inwood, NYC, on the northern tip of Manhattan.

For further titles, please visit the author's Amazon page.

tedcleary.studio@gmail.com

tedcleary.com

Made in the USA
Middletown, DE
03 November 2023

41758436R00083